PRIOR AFFAIR

A NIGHT SHIFT NOVELLA

CHRISTINA C JONES

WARM HUES CREATIVE

ONE

HAILEY

THE SMELL PULLED ME SUDDENLY, VIOLENTLY, FROM THE FULL immersion of a dream.

Whatever vivid images my mind had been creating were quickly forgotten as the rest of my senses keyed into what my nose had noticed first, and was working hard to alert the rest.

Smoke.

Bitter and acrid, all-consuming, as my eyes adjusted to the dark. Getting thicker right in front of me, making it harder and harder to breathe.

Another moment of paralyzed confusion passed before I threw back the covers to spring into action.

There was no time to bother with a robe, or shoes, none of that – just a snatch of my cell phone from the charger, and a mad dash through the house, to the kitchen. A violent cough punctuated my words as I pleaded, half-distracted, with the 911 dispatcher to send somebody.

Send... everybody?

My hands shook as I fumbled with the metal ring on the fire

extinguisher, now ignoring the dispatcher. It was her turn to plead with me – *"Ma'am, you need to get out of the house."*

She was right, of course.

I needed to get out of the house.

But I couldn't.

Not without doing... *something*.

I still hadn't seen any actual fire – just the smoke, which was getting thicker and thicker. Under the kitchen sink, I found goggles and a package of protective masks I'd purchased for a little DIY paint project I was planning.

I donned both, ended the call, and let intuition lead me to what I already knew.

It was at the front of the house.

The shitty wiring – *not* to be confused with the *original* wiring.

The house was old.

Very old.

It went all the way back – to the "free" north. It was a point of painful pride for my mother's side of the family, that my great-great-*great* grandmother had escaped the horrors of the south, and used the impeccable sewing skills she brought with her to build something that made way for a whole different kind of ownership, among a community of others who'd done the same.

Built something, in spite of.

The kind of something that sent white folks into a jealous rage, because how dare we not succumb to their cruelty? How dare we *thrive*? That was how this house had ended up lost to us in the first place, and relegated to a piece of history.

My history.

And now it was burning to the ground.

One of my biggest fears, come to life in horrifying heat and cauterizing color.

It was the damn wiring.

The electrician had stared at it for a long time, moving room to room to gaze into the holes he'd cut here and there in the walls. A long drag on the cigar hanging half out of his mouth, and then a very grave, very serious head shake.

"*You gotta get that shit outta there. Soon as possible.*"

He wasn't the only electrician who'd told me the same thing – at a similar price point – so it was nothing for me to accept his bid and schedule the work.

For next week.

Shit.

The "new" owners, at some point, had tied more modern wiring in with the old, and over the years, with every "remodel", it had been getting band aid after band aid. Jimmy – the electrician – was shocked they even had permits for it, but I'd been able to pull them. And once I told him that part, he'd shook his head again.

"*Boy they let themselves get away with doing whatever they wanna do, don't they?*"

The "*they*" was understood.

And yep, *they* sure did.

Anger and acrid smoke did a dual number on my eyes, forcing tears as I aimed the extinguisher foam at the sizzling orange flames licking up the walls. There wasn't really any furniture to speak of—the family furnishings were long gone. Even the paint and wallpaper, now bubbling and dripping to the floor, wasn't ours.

But these bones—the ones that my ancestors had saved and sacrificed to afford, that my great-great-great-grandmother and her friends and cousins and neighbors had reinforced and renovated and raised with their own hands... *those* belonged to us. Every *whoosh* of flames, every crackle, every creak, was like they themselves were screaming for their legacy to be preserved and saved. The flames seemed to have arms, hands, fingers, reaching out to me as it built, bigger and bigger.

That little fire extinguisher wasn't doing shit.

It was like every flame I snuffed produced five more – it was spreading so much faster than I could do anything about. I hopped back as the fire spread along the carpet, moving like it was following a trail of accelerant.

Rapid.

And *hot*.

So suffocatingly hot that I wanted to close my eyes, just for a second, catch my breath, and then I could — "*What the hell are you doing?!*"

An unfamiliar voice, simultaneously muffled and loud, hit my ears. Before I could even turn around, find a source, thickly gloved hands were wrapped around my biceps, pulling me backward as a stream of something much more efficient than what I'd been working with started lining the walls.

Firefighters.

"Is there anybody else in here? *Ma'am! Is there anybody else here?*"

I shook my head, through my dazed state. My ears were ringing, condensation building behind the goggles, making my field of view blurry.

Is this real? Or am I drea — "Get her the hell outta here," another voice demanded, as I suddenly realized the place was swarming with people.

"Ma'am, come on, we gotta move," a much closer voice urged – the one who'd pulled me back from the fire.

I was still clutching the – empty – fire extinguisher, my feet feeling like lead as I followed her directions toward the back door until I realized –

"I don't have on any shoes!" I screamed, suddenly panicked about the fact. "And I need clothes! And my laptop – and my—"

"*Ma'am*, I need you outta this damn house," the firefighter – a woman, demanded, practically dragging me out onto the deck, and then down the stairs as I uselessly fought against her and a peer who must've been waiting outside.

"Where's your stuff?" she asked, as the other firefighter held me to keep me from going back in. "I'll grab shoes so you won't be barefoot, and a tee shirt or something, but fuck that computer and anything else."

"It's at the back. It opens onto the deck too, right there," I told her, snatching off the mask and goggles so I could see and breathe.

She said nothing, just jogged back in as the other firefighter urged me across the yard, to where an ambulance was pulled up, waiting.

"I'm fine. *I'm fine*," I insisted, as the paramedic raised an oxygen mask to my face before I could even take the seat they offered. My insistence was emphatically ignored, and I quickly realized *I* was wrong.

I needed it.

"You know this was stupid as hell, right?" the woman from before asked, tossing a pair of tennis shoes, joggers, and a tee shirt into my lap – all the stuff I'd had set up in a chair before I went to bed, to make it easier for myself to workout in the mornings.

Who knew I'd need it for a whole other reason?

She pulled her headgear off, crossing her arms to stare me down as the paramedic strapped a blood pressure cuff on me.

I pulled the oxygen mask down so I could answer.

"I just wanted to save the house."

Those words were barely off my lips when a horrifying crash met my ears. Everybody's eyes went wide, turning toward the house, but my view was strategically blocked. I shoved away from the paramedic, stepping around the ambulance so I could see.

The whole thing was in flames.

That's how it looked to me.

An anguished scream built in my throat, but I swallowed it somehow as my eyes blurred over the sight of half the house, collapsed into... match sticks, basically.

"*Everybody got out, right?*"

"Yeah! Ellis had just cleared the back door!"

Orange smoke billowed high in the air, fading into the navy sky as I watched. It was a fittingly starless night, no beauty to contrast the ugly destruction happening on the ground as I was forced back down, onto a gurney this time.

"We're taking you to Regional, ma'am, unless you've got another preference," the paramedic explained, no preamble.

"What? No, I don't need—"

"You were in there breathing smoke a while, you've got singes on your hair, your gown, and I don't like the look of that burn on your foot – we're taking you."

There wasn't room to argue.

And really, I didn't have the energy anyway.

Whatever adrenaline rush had pulled me from the bed was wearing off now, leaving me exhausted and delirious, my head spinning as I gratefully sucked in that fresh oxygen.

One paramedic tucked my change of clothes beside me before closing the ambulance doors to pull off. My eyelids were heavy, my eyelashes leaden, and I was so drained that I stopped fighting it. I dropped a hand to my side, and it hit my cell phone, tucked there in a pocket, forgotten.

I'd laughed about pockets on a nightgown.

Why the *hell* would I ever need pockets while I was sleeping?

Now though, I was glad I'd overcome the silliness of such a feature and bought it – the fabric was pretty and soft. And it had come in handy – I had no ID, no money, but these days the next best thing, with all the convenient e-wallet features, was a cell phone.

I closed my eyes then, letting relief wash through me momentarily, before a different, sobering thought took hold.

I didn't have anybody to call.

TWO

ELLIS

"Oh thank goodness – add me to the list of people you've saved tonight," Reva gushed, reaching for the disposable coffee cup in my hand as soon as she spotted it.

"Hold up now." I turned my back to her, moving the cup out of her reach. "How do you know this is for you?"

Reva's eyes shot briefly to the ceiling. "Stop playing."

"Who? Somebody playing? I'm not playing at *all*," I grinned, sidling up closer to wrap an arm around her. "If anything, *you're* the one playing. You think I came all the way out of my way to bring you a coffee cause you're cute?"

A smile spread over *her* lips, too. "No, I think you brought it cause you *love* me," she insisted, dodging my hug but deftly retrieving the *UG* printed cup from my hand. "You know I can't stomach that Milli-Vanilli ass *City Brew* shit they stock around here. Cannot wait for that damn contract to run out."

"Huh?" My eyebrows furrowed, confused where this conversation had gone. "What contract?"

Her eyeroll was much longer – much more genuine – this time. "We *finally* got the actual story of why the hospital won't stock

Urban Grind – the previous director signed a long ass, can't get out of it contract with *City Brew* before she left for greener – *whiter* – pastures. One last *fuck you* to our Black asses before she left, I guess."

Understanding relaxed my features, and I nodded. "I see. She get a kickback from it or something?"

Reva shrugged. "Probably. But her in-laws own the company, so..."

"Right."

"Anyway—I wasn't expecting to see you tonight – figured you'd go home and knock right out."

As soon as she asked, it was as if all the fatigue of the last twenty-four hours hit me at once, making my limbs heavy. I pushed out a sigh before I gave an affirmative nod to her question. "I wanted to check in on that family from yesterday?"

"Ellis, you know I can't—"

"I know, privacy laws, I get it," I assured her, hands raised. "But can't you spare your *favorite* first-responder a little generic, non-detailed good news that could be about anybody in the world, not specific to this burn ward?"

Reva groaned, but looked around a bit before motioning with her head for me to follow her around the corner. "You make me sick."

"No I don't."

"You right." This time, her wordless communication came as a deep sigh before she met my gaze. "The mother didn't make it. Dad has a hard road ahead. But... they protected those babies. The kids will be fine. Their godparents are both here with them."

I had said nothing yet – hadn't even moved or reacted at all, actually. Still, Reva reached out with her unoccupied hand, squeezing my arm.

"Hey, it's not y'alls fault," she insisted. "The call came too late, and the fire spread too fast. There wasn't anything more y'all could do."

"Exactly the problem," I muttered, looking past her. My eyes landed on a sight that raised my brows in surprise. "What is she doing in the hall?"

Confusion twisted Reva's face for a moment before she turned, following my gaze to where a woman was seated, staring off into space.

"Oh, shit – I didn't know she was still here," Reva answered. "Her burns were minor – they only sent her back here because the ER is getting hammered. She can go home."

I shook my head. "No... she can't."

Not safely, anyway.

Last I'd seen, there was a gaping hole in the front – smaller than it would've been, if it hadn't been for a last-minute assist from the rain. It had been a long time since a house fire gave us so much trouble – it was in historic Blackwood though, so the materials differed from the stuff that met modern safety standards.

From a historical perspective, it was a loss, for sure. It was among the last original homes still standing, and one of the nicer ones, at that. If I wasn't familiar – intimately, depressingly familiar – with the unpredictable, consuming nature of fire, I'd almost understand why the woman had risked her life to save it.

Almost.

Civilians not removing themselves when they should, *while they could,* was one of the biggest contributors to negative outcomes in emergency situations. Cause then, somebody had to go get their asses.

Hopefully.

When the dispatch told us the caller who'd reported the fire was unresponsive, we'd gone in already half-somber, thinking we'd find her passed out from smoke inhalation at best, and at worst... well, that part was obvious.

What none of us had expected was to find her barefoot, barely dressed, in painting goggles, damn near surrounded by the very flames she was trying to put out.

It was foolish.

But at least she was alive.

"Hey," Reva muttered, getting my attention. "See if she needs a ride to a friend's place or something, would you? We can't have her sitting here."

Without giving me a chance to decline the request, Reva was off, happily humming as she sipped from the latte I'd brought her.

Shit.

Okay.

The woman didn't even look up as I approached – she was clearly lost in whatever thoughts she'd conjured in her mind. I had to wave a hand in front of her face to get her attention, and even then, there was such clear mystification in her eyes I wondered if maybe the hospital *was* where she needed to be.

I cleared my throat, trying not to get too distracted by those eyes – dazed, yes, but also strikingly intense as she focused on me. "Sorry to... interrupt, I guess, but um... do you need a ride or something?" I asked, feeling daft as the words left my mouth.

The question must've confused her too, because she frowned. "Do I know you?"

A dry laugh pushed from my throat. "Uh... not exactly. I'm one of the firefighters from earlier... at your house," I explained, fishing out my wallet to flash my official ID to accentuate my words.

Her eyes went wider. "My house? You were there? How... what happened? Is it... were you able to save it?"

I swallowed hard, giving myself a chance to think, even briefly, before answering her question. "A good amount of the house is still standing – it's *not* a total loss."

"So I can go back to it?"

"No," I admitted. "Not to live. Not soon."

Her gaze pinned to mine, so full of loss and pain that it made *my* damn chest hurt. Then she blinked and nodded, returning her focus to some unmarked point on the wall. "I'm not sure why I asked that. I... saw it... um... I saw the..."

"Let me give you a ride," I offered again, not wanting her to sink back into... whatever headspace she was in before. "It's late, but I'm headed out anyway – I can drop you pretty much anywhere, okay? Come on."

She held me with another long stare, but didn't argue with my offer. There were no belongings for her to grab other than the cell phone she'd been put in the ambulance with, still clutched tight in her hand as she wordlessly, aimlessly stood.

"Okay," I nodded. "Let's go."

It *was* late.

And I was exhausted.

But Reva was right, she couldn't hang out in the hospital indefinitely. And besides that... I felt bad for her.

Her...

"Hey, what's your name?" I asked, leading her out to where my truck was parked.

"Um... Hailey," she said. "Hailey Freeman."

"Ellis Boyd," I offered, extending a hand in her direction. For a second, when she didn't move, I thought she was going to leave me hanging, but then she slipped her hand into mine to return the gesture.

These are shitty circumstances for a first meeting, Ellis – that's likely the kind of thing she would've said, if she weren't still so clearly dazed.

Understandably.

But she said nothing, just shook my hand and then slipped hers away, leaving mine feeling strangely empty after.

In the truck, I waited until she was buckled into the safety belt to ask, "You wanna give me the address so I can plug it in?"

"Address? *Address.* Right. I..." she blinked several times, then let out a mirthless laugh and shook her head. "I... am clearly losing it, because... I don't have anywhere to go. I have no idea why I got in this damn truck. I'm sorry, I—"

"Hold up," I said, reaching across to stop her from unclipping her seatbelt and opening the door. "You don't have a homegirl? A cousin? A man? Hell... an ex you can tolerate for a couple days...?"

She huffed. "No. Not here. I haven't lived here very long. A week and a few days," she explained. "I left... everything."

"Oh. Damn."

"Yeah," she nodded. "So... I don't even know what I'm doing. Like... what the hell am I supposed to do right now?"

"You're asking me?"

"Yeah."

I shrugged. "Shit, I don't know... if it was me? Real talk... I'd need a damn drink."

Her gaze shifted to me, eyes wide, and she nodded. "Okay. That's where you can take me. That's where I need a ride to. Wherever I can get a damn drink."

THREE
HAILEY

"I'M *REALLY* NOT DRESSED FOR A BAR LIKE THIS," I SAID, EYES wide as we approached the glowing sign.

Night Shift.

The pale blue sign, affixed to the top corner of the building, high above street level, was a sharp contrast to the inky-blue sky, beckoning drinkers for miles. I doubted *they* were missing their underwear beneath joggers and a tee shirt, wearing sneakers with no socks, reeking of *eau de housefire*.

My hesitance made Ellis stop, turning to offer me a grin in rebuttal.

I'd bet that smile had turned plenty of well-intentioned refusals into acquiescence.

He had that vibe about him.

"We're dressed the same," he shrugged, calling my attention to where he was dressed similarly enough. The difference was the huge *BFD* emblazoned across his chest.

Blackwood Fire Department.

He motioned for me to come on, and when I didn't, he strode back in my direction, quickly covering the distance my reluctance had put between us on the sidewalk. There was a momentary fear he'd grab my hand again – that he'd send another one-sided jolt of electricity, like back in the hospital parking lot.

His hands went to my shoulders instead.

He'd stepped behind me, and with a gentle push, I was moving again – partially in compliance, and partially trying to get away from his touch.

I didn't like what it was doing to me.

There was entirely too much to consider – to plan, to fix, to pay for – with a damn *fire* taking out half the house. I still hadn't even seen it, didn't know the first thing to do after a fire, had no idea how I was going to explain this to the people who hadn't wanted me to come out here for any of this in the first place.

And what was I doing?

Walking into a bar, entirely too aware of the handsome firefighter behind me.

Inside, I quickly realized I wasn't nearly as out of place as I thought – there were a few people really *dressed,* but mostly it was a sea of *BFD, BPD, BEMS, BRH* tee shirts.

Blackwood Fire Department.
Blackwood Police Department.
Blackwood Emergency Medical Services.
Blackwood Regional Hospital.
First responders.

As soon as we stepped into the main area, a chorus of *"Boyd!"* went up, coming from seemingly all sides. His hands left my shoulders in favor of greeting his... friends, I guess. I caught a few nasty looks in the crowd, and could easily guess what those were about.

I put up a mental block to *that* energy and tuned my antennae to the bar.

He didn't even notice when I slipped away, which was fine – I was where I needed to be. His suggestion of a drink had been an excellent one, and I was all set to have the pretty bartender put something strong in front of me when I remembered... *shit*.

My purse had been right there on the table, in the now-destroyed front entryway of my house.

"Can you accept a mobile wallet payment?" I asked, holding up my phone to illustrate what I meant.

"Of course," she agreed, giving me a good reason for the relief that washed through me before she added, "but you walked in with Ellis, right? He's paying."

Immediately, I shook my head. "I don't even really – I don't know him," I explained. "I'm just... we..."

"What are you drinking?" she asked, obviously not interested in my clarification. "We've got *Rebirth, No Angel,* and *Auntie's House* on tap right now, or... you need something stronger?"

"Well," I sighed. "My house burned down tonight, so... I kinda think the stronger the better."

Her lips fell apart in a little gasp, eyes wide. "Oh, shit. I'm *so* sorry, sis."

"Yeah. Me too," I told her, blinking away the sudden urge for tears. "So um... whatever you think would work."

She nodded. "I've got you," she said, reaching *way* up to the top shelf for an expensive-looking bottle with a large *K* etched into the glass. "This one is on me – next one on Ellis," she grinned, pouring me a generous shot of what I identified as bourbon – fantastic bourbon – as soon as it hit my tongue.

I wanted to savor it; I really did.

Instead, I followed the impulse to knock it back, relishing the smoothness as it went down my throat. By the time I put the glass down on the glossy bar top, there was already another in front of me.

Good.

If I could drink away the fact that I was essentially homeless now, even momentarily... I damn sure would.

"Hold up now," Ellis' deep voice rumbled in my ear as I slid the shot toward me. A moment later, he'd taken the open seat beside me. "I thought we were supposed to be drinking together?"

"Was that the agreement?" I asked, already raising the glass to my lips, but not drinking. "You seemed busy."

"I'm here now."

"I already started."

"Even more reason to wait on me," he insisted, flagging down the same bartender from before. "What you got her drinking, Lark?"

She smirked. "Top shelf, on your dime."

"Damn, it's like that?" he chuckled, looking back and forth between the two of us. "Shit... pour me one too, I guess."

The bottle was still down, so it only took a second for him to have a glass in his hand, too. When he held it out like we were supposed to toast or something, I frowned.

"What the hell would we be drinking to? My house burned down."

He nodded, meeting my gaze. "It did. And that's messed up. But... you're here to tell the story, aren't you?"

My eyebrows shot up. "Wow. Yeah. You're right."

"That's something to drink to."

"Indeed," I agreed, tapping my shot to his. "To shifted perspectives."

He lifted an eyebrow at me, then nodded. "To shifted perspectives."

The second shot didn't go down as smooth as the first – not the fault of the liquor, though. He was staring at me as I poured the shot down my throat – not skipping a beat with his own, but making it difficult for me not to choke a bit.

I covered it well, though.

"You feel better now?" he asked, his careful attention still intensely trained on my face.

I shrugged. "Would you?"

"Not really."

"There's your answer then," I told him, eyeing my empty shot glass with such obvious disdain that it made him laugh, then flag Lark down.

"You a beer drinker?" He asked.

I frowned and shook my head. "Not in the slightest."

"I see. Let me turn you into one."

Before I could insist otherwise, he'd already asked for two glasses of some beer I was unfamiliar with, but recognized as one of the names the bartender had told me about when I first sat down.

"It's a waste of your money," I told him. "And the bartender is already giving me top shelf on your tab, remember?"

He chuckled. "I do. And who exactly decided that, by the way?"

"That's what she said."

"Then so it is," he nodded, with another easy smile.

Dangerously easy.

I knew my head shouldn't be where it was, but there wasn't much I could do about it. My brain wanted to focus on good things – like the vague familiarity of this man's appealing dark brown skin and exceptionally rideable face.

Not to mention the firefighter-standard shoulders.

The delivery of the beer was an excellent distraction, and if nothing else, I was willing to try new things. Beer was beer, but the enthusiasts of the world always thought they had the one favorite to clear all the piss-flavored brews from the memories of your past.

They never did, but...eh.

He was paying.

It was the least I could do.

"Cheers," he said, tapping his glass to mine before lifting it to his mouth for a long gulp. I was a bit more cautious with mine, not wanting to fill my mouth with an unpleasant taste...

Except...

This wasn't unpleasant at all.

It was...

"Good, isn't it?" Ellis grinned, leaning towards me a bit as a new person took over on the karaoke stage. "Not like them other motherfuckers you've dealt with, right?"

I laughed, but that was pretty accurate, and I admitted it with a nod. "It's... really complex. Bold, citrusy... kinda spicy? What *is* this?" I asked, taking another, longer sip. "It's kind of amazing."

"This is *No Angel*. Brewed right here at *Night Shift*."

"Like in this actual building?"

He nodded. "Yeah, right here."

"Okay, well, that makes this even cooler. A whole brewery, right in the middle of the city?"

"Nanobrewery," he corrected. "Black-owned."

"I've never even heard of a nanobrewery – you're kinda blowing my mind."

"Wait until I tell you that the bourbon you had first, is from the same family that owns *Night Shift*."

This was too much.

I narrowed my eyes at him, leaning in as the liquor loosened my tongue. "Is it *your* family, Ellis? Are you telling me all this to impress me, and get into my panties?"

"Nah," he laughed, "To both questions. I'm offering additional context, since you seemed interested."

"Oh. Good. I'm actually not wearing any panties anyway," I shrugged, taking another sip.

Truly, I had meant no innuendo, but the quick darkening of Ellis' eyes told me it was clearly taken in that manner. "Ms. Freeman – do I need to have the bartender cut you off?"

"No, I'm not close enough to *on my ass* yet – I need to be in *ma'am, you can't dance on the tables in this establishment* state," I declared. "For the next forty-eight hours or so, until I figure out how to tell my mother I burned down the hundred-year-old house she never wanted me to buy."

His eyes went wide. "Oh, shit. Why didn't she want you to buy it?"

I shrugged. "You try getting a straightforward answer about

anything out of Chelle Freeman when she doesn't want to talk about it. The mob would've loved her."

"Damn, like that?"

"Unfortunately," I said. "I think it's... bad memories, or something? I don't know. She's never even set foot in it though – not her, or even my grandmother."

"Wait, so it's... like an inheritance or something?"

"It should've been," I told him. "And with it back in my family's possession, I was hoping it could be again. But now..." I couldn't even finish that sentence.

Hell, the thought.

I immediately blocked it out, in favor of draining the rest of my glass.

"Hey, it's not a lost cause," Ellis said, with a gentle grab under my elbow. It was clearly meant as a comfort thing, but my body took it elsewhere – between my legs, making it hard to focus on words I really wanted to hear. "I know a great restoration company out here. It won't be cheap, but they can make it like the fire never happened. Since it's in the historic district too, you might even be able to apply for a grant from the city – get them to split some of the cost with you or something."

"That would be amazing," I huffed. "But I... I don't know. I think it's still too much to process right now."

"And you don't have to," Ellis assured. "It's a lot, definitely. Just focus on whatever can keep you grounded right now."

I scoffed. "Yeah, *grounded* is exactly where I'm not trying to be," I admitted, raising a hand to flag the bartender down.

I didn't want realism, or logic, even if it was steeped in hopefulness, not right now.

What I wanted was another damn drink.

FOUR
ELLIS

SHE DIDN'T NEED ANOTHER DRINK.

Not that it was my business if she did, but still – I met Lark's gaze as she sauntered back in our direction, silently imploring her to *not* knock this woman on her ass.

When she didn't wake up with a hangover the next morning, she'd thank me.

Lark talked her into trying another beer.

Since she liked the first one, she was gung-ho for another flavor, and I even had one with her. To further reduce the chances of her requesting another drink, I pulled her from the bar, positioning us in a tucked away corner booth.

"You know I'm not stupid, right?" she asked, meeting my gaze over the table. "I know you're trying to keep me from getting as drunk as I think I want to be."

"Is it working?"

"Barely," she admitted. "Especially since you're the one who suggested a drink."

"Yes... *a* drink. You're on number...?"

"None of your business, damn," she giggled, shaking her head.

"Do you clock the alcohol intake of everybody you pull from a fire like this?"

"Only the ones I'm trying to keep from feeling like shit tomorrow."

"As if my house burning down wasn't already going to do that?"

"Even more reason to not over indulge," I explained. "All of this is going to come into terrifying focus with the light of day. Do you *really* want to be dealing with a hangover on top of it?"

Her full lips wrinkled, thoughtfully pursed as she conceded a nod. "You're probably right. This is my first house fire – I don't really know the protocol."

"I wouldn't say there's a protocol, but... you learn some things here and there."

"As a firefighter?"

"Yeah."

"So... I defer to expert experience," she shrugged. "I'd never even used a fire extinguisher before."

My eyebrows shot up. "Really? And you just... decided to try your luck for the first time in a hundred-year-old house?"

"I have *never* been accused of cowardice," Hailey laughed. "But... yeah, I grabbed it and got into it. I'm sure I probably read the instructions when I bought the thing, but other than that? Way outside of my skill set. Had to be pure adrenaline. I'm sure *you* think I'm a maniac, who risked other lives by not saving my own instead of trying to save a house."

"Well, that's exactly what happened," I chuckled. "But... shit, I get it. And I've dealt with much more idiotic things than a homeowner with an extinguisher trying to put a fire out."

"So maybe not a maniac then?"

"Maybe."

She was at the end of her beer.

And so was I, with mine.

Which... should've marked the end of this interaction.

Instead, I leaned across the table.

"You *sure* we haven't met before?" I asked, narrowing my eyes. "I swear, I feel like... you look familiar."

She shook her head. "If we have, I don't remember, but... I kinda wondered the same thing. Maybe we saw each other in traffic one day or something," she shrugged. "Or... maybe we both have that kinda face."

"Yeah... maybe. What do you do for a living?"

Her eyes went wide, fingers tracing the top of her glass. "Uh... that's a bit of a tough question. My folks would say I'm unemployed."

"And what would *you* say?"

She smirked, and... *damn*, this was a beautiful woman. I couldn't front like I was just noticing, but it was like the longer I sat here with her, the more potent it became.

"I would say I'm a writer."

"Like, books?"

She shook her head. "No. Like... articles that may as well *be* books. Long form."

"Oh really. Who do you have bylines with?"

"All the ones you've heard of."

There was no arrogance – just a matter-of-fact statement that she was a badass.

"So... definitely *Sugar&Spice* then?"

Not a smirk this time – a smile. "I was offered an editorial position there, actually. I haven't started yet though, so..."

"*I told you not to be out there in that big city with no job, don't call me when you gotta be on the corner to pay them bills, since you wanna be grown,*" I teased, in a high-pitched voice that made her laugh.

"Oh my God – have you been bugging my phone calls with my mother?" she asked, shaking her head.

"Just channeling what I *know* the women in my family would've been on your back about," I told her, chuckling. "When do you have to start?"

"Not for another week. Thank goodness. I'm definitely going to need some time to process... all this. I'd been beating myself up for taking so long to buy furniture and all that, but now..."

"Now what?"

"Now, where was I gonna put that shit anyway?" she laughed. "If it was ordered, I'd have nowhere for it to go. If it was already delivered, it would all be ruined. So for once, dithering benefited me."

I nodded, relaxing back into the booth. The more she spoke, the more of her personality bled out, temporarily overshadowing the – understandable – melancholy from when I first approached her in the hospital hall.

"Does indecision usually go badly for you?" I asked, wanting to keep the conversation going, even though I was genuinely exhausted. End of shift was always a relief, but *this* twenty-four-hour stretch had been particularly hellish.

My bed was *calling*.

But for whatever reason... Hailey's company was speaking louder.

"No," she answered, finally pushing away her empty glass. "I rarely stand for it – especially in myself. I'm actually more of the decisive type. Not a lot of ruminating for me."

"Not a fan of gray areas?"

"I hate them – within reason. Some things require nuance, of course, but generally...choose a side. In or out. Up or down. Make a damn choice, you know?" she said. "Like... right now. I am going to stop sitting here waiting for someone to tell me what to do, and I am going to go right here on my phone, and ... book a room for the night. For five nights. Or something," she shrugged, already half-distracted by the result of whatever she'd typed. "There are a lot of damn hotels in this city, wow."

"There's a new one," I offered. "Pretty close. It's a Drake property, but not the big fancy ones – it's the little eclectic type, you know what I mean?"

"Like a boutique hotel? That's exactly what I'd prefer," she murmured, eyes on her screen. "Is it this one? *Garden of Eden* – sounds like a porn setup."

"*Wow*," I laughed.

Her eyes locked with mine, dancing with amusement. "What? Tell me you don't see it! A hotel, named after paradise..."

"I think it's like... botanical," I explained, still chuckling. I only knew about it because Reva had shoved her phone in my face one day to show me pictures, declaring I should sponsor a staycation for my "favorite nurse". "A bunch of plants all over the place, vegan restaurant, so on..."

"*Ohhhh.* That actually sounds right up my alley. Okay. Thank you, I'm gonna book it," she said.

A few moments later, she put her phone down on the table. "There. Now I have a place to sleep tonight."

"Man, so you *really* don't know anybody here?"

"I *really* don't," she countered. "Well, I know writers I've worked with who live here, and old college classmates, but somebody I can call and stay with? Nah." She stopped, then shook her head. "Wow, I am a murder-stalker's wet dream right now. New to the city, telling anybody who'll listen that no one would miss me..."

I laughed. "Well, luckily, I'm not a... did you say *murder-stalker*?"

"I did – if you were one, you'd be familiar with the term."

"I could be fronting though."

She nodded. "True. So, in that case, you should know that my vagina has teeth."

A bark of laughter had burst out of me before I could catch myself, prompting her to drop the faux serious expression and break into a giggle.

I tapped a hand on the table. "I know you meant that as a deterrent, but I'm actually pretty intrigued now, so..."

"It spits acid, too."

I cringed. "Okay *now*. That's the one you want to use. Eliminate all chances of murder-stalking."

"Perfect." There was still a smile on her face before she bit her lip. "So... I feel like this is a great time to ask if that offer to give me a ride was a onetime deal or not?" she said. "I probably shouldn't try to walk to the hotel."

"Nah, it's a bit too far for that," I said. "But yeah, I can give you a ride. That's not a problem."

Actually, it was perfect.

I needed to get some rest, and it would be much easier to do that knowing she had a safe place to lay her head.

My goodbyes were quick – I didn't want to contribute to any kind of speculation about Hailey and me, even though I wasn't naïve enough to think that wasn't already happening. In fact, it was easy to attribute her silence on the short drive to a few looks we'd gotten – and a muttered comment – from, uh... prior acquaintances in the crowd.

In fact, her first words after climbing into my truck happened a block away from the hotel, when she let out a soft curse and dropped her head into her hands.

"What's up?" I asked, concerned about her sudden shift.

She blew out a sigh, then answered. "How the hell am I gonna check into this hotel? I have a Drake properties account with my information, but I don't have any ID, no credit cards *on* me. Shit."

"Hey – don't worry about it," I told her. "I'll come in with you – maybe I'll know whoever's at the front desk, and they can do me a favor. Or, I can cover the night for you – you can probably get your stuff tomorrow."

"Wow." She looked to me, eyebrows lifted in surprise. "Um... thank you. Is this standard Blackwood Fire Department treatment? Cause I gotta say, the customer service is impeccable."

"Absolutely not," I laughed. "In fact, I am probably tapdancing all over ethics rules, but... fuck it. We're here now," I said as I pulled up to the hotel. "Let's see what happens."

What happened was, after the explaining the situation, the worker at the front desk was willing to take us at our word – with my credit card information as a contingency. Hailey had stayed at other

Drake properties before, had reward points and all that, so they weren't *too* worried about her destroying the room – or them not getting paid.

"*Let me know if you need anything else,*" I told her, once it was clear she was going to be taken care of. Then, I headed off – moving slow as shit as fatigue continued catching up to me. I'd just made it to my truck when I heard my name, and looked up to see Hailey doing a little jog in my direction.

"What's up?" I asked, concerned. "Something wrong?"

"No," she answered. "You know how I said I didn't like to spend a long time deliberating things?"

I raised an eyebrow. "Yeah... no *ruminating* with you. That's the word you used."

"Yeah," she grinned. "Well..." My other eyebrow joined the first somewhere near my hairline as she slipped what I had to assume was an extra keycard for her room into my hand. "You said to let you know if I needed anything."

I scoffed. "Yeah, but... I don't follow..."

A little smirk spread over her full lips, and she nodded. "Yes, you do."

I did.

But...

Wow.

"I'm tired, so I'm going inside," she said. "The room number is on the little envelope. I'll see you upstairs... or not."

She turned to walk off without waiting for an answer.

And since I wasn't sure about the answer anyway, I did what I was already going to do.

I climbed into my truck.

FIVE
HAILEY

WHATEVER PAIN RELIEF THEY'D GIVEN ME AT THE HOSPITAL WAS wearing off.

It had to be some weak stuff, cause I was *definitely* a little tipsy, which ideally would've meant feeling... maybe not *nothing*, but much less than this.

Shit.

Minor medication for what they'd classified a minor injury, but as I dropped to a seat on the oversized bed and peeled my shoes off, it felt anything *but*.

My poor toes.

Briefly, I closed my eyes, pushing away the nagging discomfort to look at my surroundings. As promised, the room was full of big, beautiful green plants, a nice complement to the white bedding and natural wood toned furniture.

Just looking around made me feel more at ease, and I was pleased to see— after limping to the bathroom— that the same aesthetic was continued throughout the room. My gaze landed on the fresh eucalyptus in the shower, and immediately I knew – this was the hotel of my dreams.

What a beautiful place to wash this shitty day off me.

Mentally, I took an inventory of the plants, making a game of naming the ones I recognized, and seeking the little engraved information label on the pot for the ones I didn't. There was a heaven-adjacent robe in the closet, and the linens were from the same region, it seemed.

It was all going to be quite a lovely escape.

Once I was undressed, I took one last peek at my phone. It was way too late at night – or early in the morning – for me to still be up. I was content for my mind to remain there, lambasting myself to get some rest, not trying to hang like I was still in my twenties. But then I climbed in the shower, and the hot water against my already well-done tootsies brought me crashing back into why I was in a hotel at all.

Because I didn't have anywhere *else* I could be.

... where the hell is Ellis?

That hit me like a second ton of bricks – the fact that at least twenty minutes had passed since I'd boldly slipped him a key to my room.

And he'd done *nothing* with it.

Damn.

Several questions ran through my mind, with *"Is this what rejection feels like?"* being chief among them. Frankly, it was a foreign concept to me – making it easy to brush off and focus instead on getting any residual tinges of smoke off me.

And think about what I was going to say to my mother.

"Let it rest."

That had been her constant refrain throughout this entire process, which had taken me by surprise. I wasn't even looking for the opportunity to bring our family property back into our hands- it fell into my lap with an email from Collette Cole, who'd identified herself as a "history buff". I quickly found out that she was more than that – she was Blackwood's official historian and museum curator, working with a team to preserve as much of the original city as possible.

She had a personal passion for reconnection to go with that preservation, so whenever she could, she tried to get property back into the hands it should've been in all along.

Apparently, my mother and grandmother had ignored her attempts at correspondence.

But I didn't understand how it was better to *let it rest*.

Not when I'd grown up hearing about my great-great-*great* grandmother, whose name I shared. Her legacy had been used as a lesson in independence and hard work, her accomplishments used to inspire, and her reputation used to shame.

You think Mama Hailey escaped north for you to use your freedom to put on shorts like that?

And then there was a quiet shift.

I remembered realizing one day, in my latter years of high school, that it had been a while since *WWMHD – what would Mama Hailey do?* – had been wielded against me. I'd asked what my *great*-grandmother – the one who relocated to the west coast, and was a slightly more timely historical reference point for my shorts – would think.

Mama got *very* flustered that day, mumbling something about the family-owned bridal shop, and then... nothing. From there on, she acted like she had no clue what I meant, but I thought about it, every once in a while, without bringing it up.

Noticing that neither she nor my grandmother brought her up either.

And then I got that email from Collette, and everything went nuts.

They wanted me to "let it rest" and I wouldn't.

Then they *forbade* me from buying the house, so obviously, I *had* to.

There was going to be a full-blown weekend celebration event for the *"Now look at you, looking stupid"* I had coming, in the wake of this fire.

Shit.

"Hailey?"

The unexpected tenor of Ellis' voice caught me completely off guard.

I turned in the direction of the bathroom doorway and immediately tripped over my own damn feet. Before I could truly register what was happening, I was on the shower floor, being blasted right in the face with hot water.

"Oh, shit!"

No shit.

I didn't even want to think about how ridiculous I must've looked before Ellis helped me up from the floor. I pushed my wet hair from my eyes, scrubbing a hand over my face to somewhat dry it before I could meet his gaze.

He laughed.

"This is funny to you?" I asked, tamping down the laughter that was building in *my* chest, too, now that I could breathe. "My ass hurts now."

"I'm sorry about your ass," he chuckled, reaching to shut the water off. "And I'm not laughing about you falling, it's just... there was supposed to be a whole sexy, *sorry I took so long* moment, but then you were on the floor, and I..."

"*Wow*," I droned, still trying my best not to give in as he broke into a fresh rumble of laughter. "What *did* take so long, by the way?"

"I had to go park – couldn't leave my truck in front of the building."

"Right. So that accounts for the first three to five minutes. And then...?"

"I had to figure out if coming up here was a mistake or not."

My eyebrow went up. "Why would it be a mistake?"

"Because I pulled you out of a fire less than twelve hours ago, and you've been drinking."

"Not nearly enough to be deprived of a big dick."

Ellis chuckled. "How do you know it's big?"

"Those women weren't giving me the stink-eye at the bar because of your sparkling wit and personality," I answered, swiping away fresh rivulets of water from my hair before they could get into my eyes.

"You saying I don't have those?"

"I'm saying they weren't invited to this hotel room."

He smirked. "That's hurtful."

"No it's not," I laughed, finally collecting enough balance to feel secure about it when I pressed my body, soaking wet, against his. "You told me to let you know if I needed something. So I did. Now are you going to do something about it?"

My eyelids fluttered closed as Ellis' fingers went to the back of my neck, his thumb skimming down my throat.

"You gonna be specific?" he asked, and I shook my head before I met his gaze.

"Figure it out."

He answered my demand with another confident smirk that sent a shiver of arousal up my spine as his fingers crept up into my hair. I expected some sort of rebuttal, some smart remark, but none came — what I got instead was his lips against mine, and then his tongue in my mouth.

I was crossing all sorts of new thresholds.

I didn't kiss strangers.

I didn't let them lead.

Historically, both had led to disappointment, so I'd taken charge — *your mouth can go anywhere except my mouth, I'll tell you where you can put your dick and you better listen, you make **me** cum **first**, condoms are non-negotiable.*

Those standards ensured an enjoyable time for all parties, and helped dissuade from the illusion of intimacy, since that wasn't the goal.

Ever.

But Ellis' tongue in my mouth, his hands gripping my thighs as he easily hauled my legs around his waist to carry me back into the bedroom... neither of those things felt impersonal.

In fact, his touch was... something else entirely that I couldn't pinpoint.

Usually, I'd lower the lights.

To preserve the fantasy, you know?

In the dark, I was whoever, and he was whoever. Flaws were too obscured in shadows to be a distraction, or even matter. And... I didn't need visibility reminding me that what I was doing was risky, that I barely knew more about my bed partner than his name.

If it was even real.

Tonight, warm light spilled from a series of wood sconces lining the room, bathing everything in a dreamy sort of glow. No surface, including the expanse of my skin as Ellis laid me across the bed, was left untouched.

I couldn't hide.

Didn't want to.

Ellis' greedy visual appraisal felt more like a reunion than discovery, prompting me to spread my legs open, wantonly wide. I watched his face – the parting of his lips, the darkening of his eyes – as he climbed onto the bed with me, still dressed. When he lowered his head to kiss the soft insides of my thighs, I gasped.

There was no thrill of the first touch of his lips to my skin.

No anticipatory rush of stimulation.

It wasn't foreign.

It was... a revival.

Reunification.

Which was *crazy*.

I'd never met this man before tonight, never seen his face or heard his name.

A minor fact that did nothing to impede Ellis greeting my pussy like a friend he'd known forever, and thought about every day. There was nothing timid or uncertain about the way he buried his face between my open thighs, treating me to long, slow laps of his tongue. With one hand, I gripped a handful of the lush white duvet, the other went to his head for encouragement, not direction.

He needed none.

An arm braced around my thigh to keep me open to him, thick fingers in my pussy to slow stroke and tease, his tongue poised for intimate attention to my clit... Ellis knew *exactly* what he was doing. I closed my eyes, ignoring the pain as my toes clenched in pleasure, back arched off the bed. There wasn't a single huff or word of scolding – he moved with me, never backing off, never giving me a moment to come down – he kept pushing me higher.

Higher.

Higher.

Until there was no coming down, and I didn't want to anyway, because there was perfection right where I was, with Ellis still devouring me as I came. When he finally released my trembling thighs to undress, I should've reminded him about protection.

But how could I, with a bizarre sense of intimacy telling me there was no need for it?

Ellis was naked now – beautifully.

He reached for his pants to get his wallet.

He opened the wallet, then looked at me.

And decided.

A wordless, *stupid*, deeply satisfying, skin-to-skin decision that felt like the only real possibility.

His dick was made for me.

That was the only explanation for how neatly he sank into my body, perfectly long, perfectly thick. His lips came to my lips, chest pressed to my chest, hips meeting my hips with every stroke.

No illusions at all.

This was ... intimate.

More than it should have possibly been with a stranger.

But there was ... still this disconcerting feeling that he wasn't *that*, even though I wasn't losing my mind.

I did *not* know this man – knowledge that was a stark contrast to him fucking me like he knew me *very* well. Deep, slow strokes with my legs hiked around his waist, then up on his shoulders.

His hands on my hips, fingers digging into my flesh for encouragement as I rode him, hard.

Intense, blissful strokes from behind, with his hand wrapped around my neck.

Shit I never, *ever* did, with a stranger or otherwise, but with Ellis at the helm, fucking me into a puddle of ecstasy, I was ... in paradise.

His mouth came to my ear, nibbling me there before he shifted his tempo – from hard and fast to torturously, delightfully measured. "Is this what you needed?" he asked, as his hand slipped between my legs.

My lips parted for an answer, but none came – just a gasp of pleasure as he filled me to the brim with a sudden stroke.

"Answer the question, Hailey," he demanded, pinching my clit between his fingers. My pussy clenched hard around him, making him groan in my ear, then ask again, punctuating each word with a stroke, with the same pressure still on my clit. "*This. Is. What. You. Needed. Right?*"

"*Yesssssss,*" I whined, barely keeping myself up on my hands and knees as my answer prompted him to stroke me harder, faster, *deeper*. When my arms gave out, it didn't matter – his hands came to my breasts, pinching my nipples as he drove into me.

Again.

And again.

And again.

Yes.

Yes.

Fuck, yessss.

When I came, it was hard, and loud, and... *vivid.* He kept stroking, dropping a hand between my legs for clitoral stimulation that prolonged the blinding, deafening, paralyzing haze of an orgasm that seemed to keep going, and going, and ... *going.*

Even after he'd emptied himself inside me, and collapsed on top of me, my body was still on high alert – still aroused, still wanting more of him.

Fatigue won.

Before I could consider any implications of him staying, he was already asleep... and I was too exhausted to do anything but join him in slumber.

SIX

ELLIS

I'D LOST MY MIND.

Truly.

What else could explain waking up in a hotel room naked as the day I was born, with an equally naked damn-near stranger tangled in the sheets with me? There was actually a moment where I wondered if I was dreaming – the sun coming in through the window shades had everything bathed in a soft glow that contributed to the surreal aesthetic.

But then Hailey stirred, a delicate groan pushing from her throat as she nudged her body against me. I watched her, transfixed, as she nestled in closer, eyes still closed, and let her hand drift down to my exposed dick.

I closed my eyes as her fingers wrapped around it and squeezed – I was already hard, which was going to make it difficult to make a wise decision.

The bed shifted as Hailey moved, lifting herself over me.

Shiiiiit.

Okay.

Impossible to make a wise decision while I was buried in the invitingly saturated depths of her pussy. I peeled my eyelids open to watch her as she moved – hands anchored on my chest, eyes still closed, in her own world as she circled her hips down to mine.

I loved watching her like this.

A revelation that made me blink, because... *what?*

Why would that even cross my mind?

It was hard to dwell on the perplexing nature of a notion like that, though, when the reality – what I could literally reach out and touch —felt so impossibly damn good. The allure of all that beautiful, deep brown skin was excruciating to resist.

I *had* to touch her, had to get closer, had to sit up to taste the sweetness of her breasts, her neck...

This was insane.

I was perfectly *clear* on that.

Other things were much more clouded.

Such as the line between the casual encounter, which I was admittedly familiar with, and... whatever this was. Hailey's hands came to my face, lifting my chin as she lowered hers to press her lips to mine, mouths closed, lingering.

Losing her rhythm.

"*Ellis, please,*" she murmured against my mouth, then dropped her head to nuzzle my neck and repeat the same ambiguous request. Another vaguely breathless, "*Please.*"

I understood it perfectly.

I flipped us over, never straying from the welcoming confines of her pussy as I settled between her thighs and started moving.

Make me cum – the unspoken words that accompanied that "*please*".

Of course I would.

I'd give her anything she asked for.

Another *foolish* thought, but I couldn't focus on it.

Driving further, faster, harder, producing that delicious friction that would propel *her* into something insanity-adjacent... that was much more pertinent right now.

The sudden tension in her stomach, the involuntary vibration of her thighs, my name dripping off her lips in a steady chorus with *yes* in varying modulations as the only other lyric...

Mission accomplished.

And it wasn't a one-way street – *her* pleasure spurred mine, and I was right there with her, being wrung out by an orgasm that seemed to drain away all the troubles of the world.

At least for the moment.

"*Good morning,*" she murmured, once we'd caught our breaths, and feeling had returned to our limbs.

I gave her the same words in return, then watched as she peeled herself up from the bed to pad into the bathroom.

My cue.

I didn't rush because I wasn't trying to sneak out – it was time to go, though. I'd located the last article of my clothing to add to my pile of belongings when the bathroom door opened and she stepped out.

No eye contact.

Which was... *comforting*, strangely enough.

It let me know I wasn't imagining how disturbingly enjoyable all this had been – a paradox of feelings that made conversation difficult. I relieved my bladder in the bathroom, using the time between the toilet and walking out with clean hands to wrack my brain for what I should say to her.

"You should call the restoration company *before* you go by your house."

Was where I landed.

She was at the window, wrapped in a robe that clung to her curves in some places, flowed in others. She looked comfortable.

My words made her raise an eyebrow, though.

"Why? I need to get some of my stuff so I can live, and work. And probably get out whatever I can save – between the fire and then the rain... I'm sure it's a disaster."

I nodded, moving to my clothes to get dressed. "Which is why you should have someone with you," I explained. "It won't be the same as having a friend or something along, but they'll be able to give you some... balance. Knowing what the house means to you, I think it'll help. A lot."

"Thank you."

"You're welcome." I pulled my tee shirt over my head, then brought my gaze back to hers. "How are you this morning? With... everything?"

A soft smile spread across her lips. "I'm... as well as could be expected, I think. I'm about to use the last of my cell battery to order a toothbrush, a comb, a phone charger, panties, and breakfast to be delivered to me here," she told me, her words buoyed by a soft chuckle. "Once I have all that... I think I'll be okay."

"Good."

I should've said more.

Wanted to say more.

But how the fuck was I supposed to articulate "*Are you sure we haven't known each other – loved each other – forever? Cause the sex sure felt like it.*" without risking institutionalization?

I didn't try.

"I'm gonna head out," I told her, bending to put my shoes on.

"Thank you for last night," she said, following me to the door. "For putting me out of a blazing fire, and giving me a ride, and buying my drinks, and... damn, you did a lot," she laughed. "All that *and* you made me cum. And you're even leaving on your own."

I chuckled. "Yeah, I've never been one to push an invitation past where it needs to go," I said, stepping into the hall. "You're welcome."

I wanted to kiss her goodbye.

And... I think she wanted me to.

Instead, we exchanged awkward smiles, and she closed the door, and I headed back down to my truck, so I could take my ass home.

To reevaluate my whole damn life.

Twenty-four-hour shifts were hard on anybody.

Everybody.

Sure, we took it in stride – something that came with the territory of being members of Blackwood's Fire and Rescue team. But there was no denying the toll it took on every one of us.

The mental exhaustion, the physical exhaustion, and the least popular topic among us – the emotional exhaustion. *Every* twenty-four-hour shift was a journey, especially in a city like Blackwood, where there was almost always *something* going on.

Years back, I did a sort of ambassador program out in Sugar Valley – much smaller, up in the mountains. From day to day, even week to week, there might not be a single fire or critical emergency at all.

The nights were quiet, the days were slow.

Peaceful.

But when it was bad out there?

It was awful.

A forest fire in the middle of the night, no warning. Houses dotted all over the place, phone lines down and no cell service to notify people it was coming. Speeding through the night, trying to warn people that a miles-wide inferno was headed in their direction, swallowing everything it touched.

Literal hell.

Here in the city, things were typically more... balanced.

I wasn't sure which I preferred – if there was a preference to be had.

Every shift was a wide-ranging roller coaster of epinephrine and emotion.

Pulling some kid's puppy, unharmed, from a storm drain for breakfast. A multi-car pileup for lunch. Managing a hazardous waste spill for dinner. Rescue and recovery from an apartment blaze for bitter ass dessert.

Every time I rolled up to Station 34, there was truly no telling what I'd see that day. It always came down to a dice roll – an exhausting roulette that usually left me too wrung out to think straight. By the time I'd checked in with Reva at the hospital, which I did on most days, then swung through *Night Shift* to have a drink or two with my people – not as often as I checked in with Reva, but often enough – I was running on fumes.

So really... when I thought about it—it made perfect sense that my decision-making skills were sorely lacking.

And I absolutely thought about it, hard as hell, once I'd take my ass home, showered, and slept another ten hours after my little rendezvous with Miss Hailey Freeman, with sex having added to my exhaustion.

I was thinking harder than a motherfucker.

Trying to figure out what on *Earth* had compelled me to do something like that, and why it had felt nowhere near as wrong as I knew it should.

It wasn't like I was some paragon of celibacy, by any stretch of imagination. I wasn't saving myself for marriage, or even commitment honestly.

I had *some* standards though.

Knowing a woman's first and last name, knowing said name for at least twenty-four to forty-eight hours, and the use of protection wasn't even a question.

It was an absolute.

However.

Somehow, Hailey Freeman had taken a sledgehammer to every constant I'd previously come to depend on, and the fact remained... I barely knew the woman.

Despite the very *known each other for years* energy we'd inexplicably had.

Baffling.

I had forty-eight hours off work between shifts, and I spent an embarrassing number of them this time around thinking through that whole interaction with Hailey.

And yet, made no strides to get back in touch with women herself.

I realized later that we never did actually exchange numbers or any type of contact information. I knew she was starting a job with *Sugar&Spice* though, and... I guess I technically knew her address.

And I still had a key to her room.

But... even with me making a point of imploring her to let me know if she needed anything else, I hadn't taken that additional step. So how the hell was she supposed to get in touch?

I didn't know if she was doing okay, or if she'd followed my advice to contact the restoration company or not.

Not that I was really trying to find out.

I needed to separate myself from the situation while I puzzled through it all in my mind. Hell, I probably needed to separate myself from it, *period*.

I'd forced myself to go on about my usual sort of routine, making my way to Reva's preferred Urban Grind location so I could grab her favorite drink.

Actually... her *favorite* was the flagship store over in the Heights, but if I'd gone all the way over there, there was no way it wouldn't be cold when I got back to her.

So her second favorite would have to do.

I'd pulled out of the drive-thru with her drink and one for myself, and was headed up the street when something caught my eye. Something that made me pull into the nearest parking lot and hop out of my truck, backtracking to the sidewalk bench where I'd spotted a familiar face.

One I hadn't seen in a while.

"Franklin!" I called out as I approached, and the older man jolted up as if I was waking him from a slumber.

That was exactly why I had called out to him first, to get his attention.

Franklin didn't like being snuck up on.

"Where you been?" I asked him, dropping to the bench beside him. "I haven't seen you in at least a month or two."

"In my skin," he answered, in his usual gruff manner. "Who wants to know?"

"*I* wanna know," I chuckled. "Just trying to make sure you're doing alright."

"I'm doing just fine. Why are you in my business, young man?"

I shook my head. "I'm checking in, Franklin. Where've you been staying?"

I knew the question was going to get me further accused of being in his business, but I couldn't walk away without asking. Not when his clothes carried the distinct staleness and rumpled appearance of having been slept in over and over.

Maybe on the street.

"Why you so concerned?" he asked.

"Why wouldn't I be?" I countered. "The weather got a little rough last night – been rough for days, storming and shit. Am I wrong for wanting to know you've got a roof over your head at night?"

"You ain't gotta check on me, like I'm not a grown ass man. I take care of myself, that's all you need to know."

"Hey," I said, raising my hands. "No harm meant, you know that. You should talk to the people at Heritage House though. You know, they worked with the city to get that apartment building in the historic district fixed up. Free housing. Clean, safe, you can come and go as you please... it could be good for you."

"*Fixed up,*" Franklin scoffed. "Niggas gentrifying worse than those white folks ever did. At least the white folks didn't pretend to give a fuck, they just did what they was gone do. These other folks come along talking about they wanna help – help my ass. They wanna *clean up the streets*. Clean *us* off the streets. Well I ain't a goddamn piece of chewed up gum."

"They're not like that man, forreal," I assured him. "I ain't saying everybody that's out here "revitalizing the community" is cool, but the Heritage House people are, we've worked with them for outreach stuff. And, for the record – *I'm* not worried about the aesthetics. I'm worried about *you*."

"Worry about yourself," he demanded, shaking his head. "You still running around putting out fires for these people? Being a *hero*?" he added, with a distinct bitter edge.

"I am," I told him. "Have you talked to somebody about the stack of pension checks that ought to be waiting for you, from when you were doing it?"

"*Hell* no! So I can have motherfuckers tracking me down? Naw. I'on trust 'em."

"Not even family?" I asked.

He looked at me for a long time, then scoffed. "I *barely* trust you," he told me. "Now gone on."

That was my cue.

But before I moved on, I opened my wallet, peeling off a few twenties to put in his hand. "Get yourself something to eat," I told him. "And go talk to the people at Heritage House," I added, walking away before he could tell me to fuck off.

Back in my truck, I took a sip from my drink, frowning at the lukewarm state of it.

Reva's latte was *definitely* going to be cold.

When I arrived at the hospital though, she was too frazzled to care, she just thanked me, took a sip, then put it back in my hand as she rushed off to check on a patient. A few moments later, she was back, taking the cup from my hand for real this time, for a longer sip.

"As always – *thank* you."

"You're welcome – looks like you needed it," I added, chuckling at the dramatic-ass sips she was taking from that cold-ass cup.

"When do I not?" she countered, shaking her head. "What's up with you? You look like you've seen a ghost or something."

Shit.

I hadn't realized it was on my face, but I immediately tried to shake off whatever she was picking up on. "No idea what you're talking about."

"You're a horrible liar, Ellis – spit it out."

I sighed. "You don't need that shit right now – we'll talk after your shift."

"By the time I'm off, you'll be back on – and this is wasting time," she insisted. "What's up?"

Shaking my head, I fixed my gaze on a point down the hall before I told her. "I saw Franklin."

She didn't drop her cup.

Her hands started shaking, but she quickly pulled herself together with a curt nod. "So he's alive, then."

"Yeah. I slipped him a few dollars."

"For *what*?" she snapped, nostrils flared. "I thought we all agreed we weren't enabling him."

"Sixty dollars ain't enabling shit but a couple of meals," I replied. "He didn't look great, so..."

"He hasn't *looked great* in twenty damn years!" Reva clamped a hand over her mouth, trying to reel her emotions in – exactly the outcome I was trying to avoid.

But...

"He's my uncle, Ree. *Your*—"

"He ain't *shit* to me," she interrupted, hand raised. "Don't even say it. Just go."

"Ree..."

"I've got patients to tend to," she muttered, dropping the coffee in a nearby trash can before she headed off to the nurse's station.

I blew out a sigh, cause it was all I *could* do, really.

I wasn't about to chase her down and make her talk, so I moved on, heading for the elevator so I could leave the hospital. I only had a few hours before I needed to take my ass to bed to prepare for my next shift.

In the meantime, I needed an escape.

And I knew exactly where to go to get it.

SEVEN

HAILEY

IT WAS DIFFICULT TO LOOK AT THE HOUSE NOW.

Damn near impossible, really.

Someone from the restoration company – Angela – had shown up after my call, accompanying me to the ruins. She'd been the one to call for someone from the fire department to escort us into the safe parts of the structure, to get what few items could be saved.

Mostly just my laptop, which still smelled of smoke, days later.

I threw all the clothes and shoes away.

Not that there was much to start with.

Before coming to Blackwood, I'd been a nomad anyway – an undesirable trait my mother swore I'd inherited from the other person who contributed to my DNA.

My father.

What I wouldn't give to call *him* now – he'd likely have more jokes than solutions, but even that would give this whole situation some much-needed balance.

Right now, I literally had nothing but the hastily chosen brand new clothes on my back and a few small electronics. My hair was a wreck, I didn't have a place to live, and the job I was supposed to start soon?

I already had an impending deadline.

This is too much.

But... it wasn't more than I could handle – at least, that's what I told myself as a week after the fire, I approved the deposit for *Revival Blackwood* to... revive my house.

"I'm going to be honest with you, Ms. Freeman – we have to tear it all down. This is a demolition and rebuild."

That had hurt to hear.

Actually... *hurt* was an understatement.

It was devastating.

But rather than cry in front of a stranger, I'd taken a couple of deep breaths and swallowed my emotions, tuning my ears to hear the *rest* of Angela's words.

"...pull up the old foundation and pour a new one...frame it out... safe wiring..."

Lots of words.

Lots of *money.*

At this point, I had no clue if the home insurance would actually pay out or not, but luckily, my "rolling stone" father had left me more than alone.

He left money.

Using the inherited resources of a man she despised to rebuild *her* ancestral home was going to spark a level of passive aggressive petty I'd never seen before in my mother, I was sure.

But.

I'd committed to spending a year here, to do what I came to do, which was restoring the *original* Hailey Freeman's home to former glory.

There would just be a lot more brand-new materials involved this time.

"We can build from the original plans," Angela told me, as a consolation. *"And there are so many ingredients here, lots of brick, and*

*stone, that we can use. Even some of the wood, we can make into
shelving, use for trim work. We can weave so much of the original
house into the new, that no matter where you look, you're looking at
something hand-picked by your ancestors."*

That helped.

It *really* did.

And yet... looking at the house I'd come here for with the doors
and shutters charred to nothing, the warm red bricks marred by thick
black streaks of soot, the windows all blown out from the heat, the
wood framing underneath it all jutting at haphazard angles...

Crushing.

Really, it was hard to breathe.

There was a park across the street, so that's where I sat, with a
camera set up and my mesquite-scented laptop as a crew demolished
what was left, and saved what items they could. I was recording it all,
in words and footage, because I was still a writer, after all. And as
painful as it was, it would be a shame to walk away from such a story.

Maybe that's when my mother would find all this out.

She hadn't *asked* me to keep her updated. In fact, she'd insisted
on not wanting to hear about it, digging into her rejection of the
whole idea with sharp claws. It was as if she didn't know me at all,
because of course that made me want to do it even more, made me ask
more questions that all got shot down.

A long, *long* time ago, before I even knew what the word meant,
I'd earned the nickname of *kitten*. Not because I was particularly
small, or even that cute – I was both things, but that was beside the
point.

Curiosity killed the cat, but I was a little girl, so... kitten.

There was a marked difference in the response to my undying
need to know things – my father called it inquisitiveness; my mother
said my *lil ass was nosy*. Either way, there was no point in trying to
keep things from me. If I was interested enough, I was going to
find out.

Before now, this whole *History of Hailey Freeman* – the working title of my article – thing had been buried at the back of my mind. I had more exciting stories to chase, sex to have, food to try, a name to make for myself.

One that would make my *namesakes* proud.

And I'd done that, I felt.

No problem.

Then I got an email from someone who wanted to reconnect me with my history in Blackwood, and I couldn't think of a single more important thing.

Even *with* my mother and grandmother turning up their noses.

I watched all the processes happening with the house until my batteries were all drained, and then set off on my walk back to the hotel, which was a few blocks away. It gave me a chance to breathe in the sights and sounds of the city, and my imagination took me down the inevitable path of wondering what a moment like this may have been like for the *original* Hailey.

I knew from my initial perusal that *Blackwood* was originally known as *Sugarleaf Township* – an interesting connection between here and Sugar Valley. The maple forest had stretched all the way here, providing scenery, shelter, and resources for those first settlers. As it grew, the trees slowly disappeared, the *township* was dropped, and it was simply known as *Sugarleaf*.

Until it was half burned down.

The buildings I was walking past now were built on the graves of what had been here before. But if I tapped in far enough, my imagination could rebuild the original storefronts built from nothing, the buggies, the horses, the brick-paved roads.

The people.

I stopped at a commemorative plaque set into the stucco of one storefront, a thread of anger building in my chest as I took in the words. The monument wasn't very old – added shortly after newly elected Black leadership renamed the city. A memorial to the two generations of one family, wiped out in what had been their home, in that space.

The intruders who claimed it for themselves had turned into an ice cream shop.

It was a family therapy center now.

Which... still somehow didn't feel right, but was better than what was there before, and was at least what their descendants chose. All of this history... it was necessary, but so heartbreakingly ugly.

I stopped at every similar plaque I saw, taking it all in. I took notes of people I wanted to look further into, events I wanted to know more about. And by the time I made it back to the hotel, I was as drained as all my electronics.

After a long, hot shower, sleep came easily, even though it was too early for bed. I woke up with my energy restored, but my mind and body feeling restless. I knew hunger was probably a factor as well, so I took myself to *Arcadia*, Eden's vegan onsite restaurant, to replenish while I responded to texts from a few concerned friends.

Well... concerned was an understatement.

Partially because I had told no one the real, full extent of my "running into a few issues with the house". I didn't need any pity, and was even *less* interested in reliving any of it beyond what I would do for the article.

So I was doing my level best to shoulder it all on my own.

Anyway, the friends who'd checked on me were certainly worthy of the title, but they weren't like *that* kind of friend. Because of my travels, because of my profession, because of what others called my "brilliance", I attracted people wherever I went.

People I kept at arm's length.

I was the girl you wanted to have drinks with, and kick it. I was loads of fun on a girls' trip – impulsive enough to encourage your shenanigans, but responsible enough to make sure you made it back home unscathed afterward. You invited me to your wedding knowing I wouldn't show, but I put a dent in your registry to make up for my absence.

Hell, you could even call me if you needed a ride to or from the airport, or needed to borrow money. I wasn't above the shitty tasks no one else wanted.

But a shoulder to cry on after a tough break up?

Someone to sit in the hospital with you while you were sick?

Wrong bitch.

Not that I wouldn't do those things, it was more that... nobody looked to me for it because I had never stayed in one place long enough, never made myself available enough to cultivate that kind of relationship.

And...I couldn't – *wouldn't* – expect that kind of support from other people either.

I'd built the kind of life that rarely required it.

"Life on the fringes" was how my father had referred to it, not long before he moved on to the next plane. He fucked up with that, because even though he'd meant it as a wake-up call sort of insult, I... actually kinda like the sound of.

Like it or not, the shit fit.

I returned all those texts with enough information to assure my friends I was fine, because I was. I wouldn't blatantly lie or ignore the texts, because I wasn't a *shitty* friend.

Just a fringe one.

Damn...

Usually this was something that didn't bother me, but after spending a good part of my afternoon reading about descendants and legacies and all that, *"Who will remember you when you're not here anymore?"* type rhetoric... I don't know.

It didn't sit quite as well as it used to.

This was one thing on a miniscule list of things my parents agreed on, that at some point I might come to regret my loner lifestyle.

Of course, my father wanted me to have a full life surrounded by people I loved, who loved me back. My mother, on the other hand, was lamenting the impossibility of grandkids.

Strange, when one considered the extreme vanity of a sixty-something woman who insisted she looked young enough to be my sister.

She wasn't wrong, but I'd never tell her that, because she'd been *so* shitty after my last breakup, I refused to give her any compliments she fished for.

Petty?

Sure.

But so were her "cat lady" and "geriatric pregnancy" quips, and she wasn't cutting those out anytime soon, since she hadn't yet disabused herself of the notion that I would ever give birth to a child *anyway*.

Not with *this* pussy.

And she got mad when I asked if she was volunteering hers, so my fertile cousins' offspring would have to fulfill all her cuddling needs, or whatever the hell the interest in babies was. They were building out families, and their families were beautiful – actually, that's probably what my mother's grievance was.

Besides the fact that my complete disinterest in babymaking – and the wedding that was "supposed" to come first was ruining *Freeman Bridal's* chance to finally dress a bride that was actually family.

Her brother had multiple grandchildren, since my cousins had done plenty of that babymaking to carry on the Freeman name.

I was perfectly content with my "auntie" status though.

Yes, I could hold the baby while you fixed your plate and ate.

Yes, Tee-Tee Hailey can do bubbles with you.

No, she does not want to do a TikTok dance with you, but she'll hold the camera and get you some angles.

Yes, you can have a sip of Tee-Tee's drink.

I chuckled at the memory of that last family reunion – I'd made the block a little hot with Mama and Granny with that one, but nobody else had tripped about it. I picked up my water glass, wishing it were a *drink* as I tried to swallow the sudden sadness of never being able to host a family get-together of my own in the original house here in Blackwood.

It would be rebuilt, but *still*.

I had a hard time believing it would really be the same.

Even with what the company had said about refurbishing the old materials, even with the recovery of the original blueprints, even with the photo albums the historian could hopefully dig up for me.

It made it sting *less*, sure, but I'd rather there be no sting at all.

Shit.

I'd ended up preferring sobriety since the night of the fire – considering the face down, ass up, situation I'd wound up in after – but now I was over it. After such a taxing day – a proper drink would be a nice numbing agent.

If Arcadia's bar hadn't already closed for the night.

Or if they had mini bars in the rooms.

That series of unfortunate revelations led me into the rideshare app on my phone, updating it to reflect my current residence in Blackwood.

I needed a ride to *Night Shift*.

Just because it was a bar that was reasonably close, and one I'd been to, so I was familiar with it.

There wasn't any part of me that wanted to run into a certain bigdicked firefighter.

Really.

In fact, when I walked up to the bar and got an immediate smile of recognition from one bartender – the same one who'd served me last time – I was sorely tempted to walk out.

Maybe *after* one of those beers…

I took a seat, then waited for her – *Lark*, if I remembered correctly – to finish with what she was already doing and make her way down to me.

"You were here with Ellis a few days back, right?" she asked, obviously trying to place me.

"Um... like a week, but yeah. That's me. Can I get a... it was something with *Angel*..."

She grinned. "A *No Angel* – we finished the keg, so it's off tap, but I can get you a bottle. Or let you try something new, if Ellis hasn't already done the whole sampler flight with you."

I shook my head. "No, a bottle is fine."

"No problem," she replied, then went off to get it. She was back a moment later with a bottle opener to pull the cap off for me. "He'll probably be back before you're done with it."

My eyebrows shot up. "Huh?"

"Ellis," she explained. "He went in the back to check on the tanks, but he should be done soon."

I shook my head, eyes wide. "I..."

"You... are *not* here to meet him, are you?" she asked, cringing a bit.

"No," I replied. "It's not... *we're* not... he's more of a... casual acquaintance."

And honestly, even that was pushing it.

Lark's eyes had gone wide halfway through my sentence, for reasons that weren't clear until a hand pressed to the small of my back, *without* giving me the urge to pull away.

Shit.

"If what we did was casual, I'd love to know what you consider formal," Ellis spoke into my ear, just loud enough for my hearing, and no one else's. "I'll have one too," he told Lark, taking the empty seat beside me in a repeat of the first night he brought me here.

"I didn't come here for this," I insistently offered, torn between staying where I was and bolting.

The look on his face kept me in my seat.

"Did I say you did?" he asked, accepting the beer from Lark, who immediately went back to the other end of the bar instead of lingering like I wanted her to, so I'd have some sort of buffer.

"You don't have to say it – you're thinking it," I told him, even though I didn't really know if that was true. "I won't come back, since this is your spot. I just wanted another beer."

"Your disdain for gray areas has you making unnecessary concessions, Hailey. I'm not bothered by you showing up here."

I raised an eyebrow. "So you're *not* thinking you dicked me into stalker behavior, and I showed up because I had to have another taste?"

He ran his tongue over his lips, then smirked. "I'm thinking you wouldn't be the first. *If* that were the case. Is that what this is? You need me to fuck you again?"

Yes.

Maybe?

Definitely.

"Wow – you're showing me a bit of a different side to you tonight, huh?" I asked, shifting to squeeze my thighs together – an attempt to quiet the pleas from between my legs before he heard them.

A shrug. "I contain multitudes. Tonight – I'm in a shitty mood. Too shitty to be charming."

"What's the reason for the shitty mood?"

"Preventable death."

My lips parted in a hitched breath before I could catch myself. But then... "Oh. I'm sorry."

"Don't be. Not your fault. Not your problem. Besides... I'm a *casual acquaintance*, remember?"

"Did that hurt your feelings?"

"A little," he answered, with a smirk that contradicted his words. "That was a weird night."

"Weird?"

"Interesting."

"Interesting?"

"Remarkable."

"That's better," I said, taking a long swig from my beer. "But... it *was* weird too."

"So you admit it?"

"I never denied it," I countered, looking him right in the face. "I was making sure that was the term you wanted to use."

"Stop fucking with me," he said, with a gruff edge that made me pitifully wetter. "You're *sure* we hadn't met before?"

"Yes, *shit*," I laughed, then shrugged. "Maybe in another lifetime or something."

He chuckled, leaning into my space before he spoke. "You think us meeting in another lifetime is why I'm having a hard time not bending you over this bar?"

All the moisture from my mouth pooled in one spot, and I swallowed hard. "Multitudes, huh?"

"Yeah."

"I'm gonna go."

More like I *had* to go, because I wasn't sure the light-washed jeans I was wearing could handle a wet spot. Ellis didn't give me anything more than a grunt, which probably should've been offensive or something, but... it wasn't.

"You're paying for my beer," I told him, right in his ear, and he grinned. "And I'm still in the same room. That key should still work."

"What makes you think I still have it?"

I smirked.

He still had it.

"Pussy closes at eleven," I said, instead of answering his question.

He held my gaze for another moment, then nodded.

"I'll be there before last call."

EIGHT
ELLIS

It was late or early, depending on your point of view on three in the morning.

And shit was definitely weird.

That was *truly* the best way to describe it — the word that encompassed it all. It fit the perplexing nature of my absolute comfort stretched across Hailey's bed. Especially considering that she wasn't even in it.

We'd fucked, we'd slept, and now Hailey was at the acrylic desk across the room, her nails making a soft click-clack against the keys as her fingers flew, the glow from her screen providing the only bit of light.

She hadn't woken me up — the nightmare had.

Indistinguishable voices calling to me for help through layer after layer of rubble and debris I couldn't seem to dig through, though I'd ripped through my gloves, through my flesh, down to the bone, desperately trying.

Her fingers flying over the keys had grounded me back in reality when I startled awake, giving me something to focus on as I transitioned through that veil between conscious and asleep, into full cognizance.

Now I was tired of watching.

I needed to engage.

"How are things coming along with the house?" I asked her, breaking the relative silence.

I half expected the sound of my voice to surprise her, since she was so keenly in tune with whatever words she was pulling from her head to leave on the screen. But she didn't flinch, just turned in my direction to peer at me. I doubted she could see me well with most of the room shrouded in darkness, but somehow, she looked me right in the eyes.

"Don't you have somewhere to be?"

"Well *damn*," I chuckled, grunting a bit as I pulled myself into a position to sit up. "I take it that's your way of telling me to leave?"

"If I wanted you to leave, I would have said that," she countered. "It's an honest question. I would have expected you to go back to your own bed after we were done. Instead, you fell asleep."

"What if I like this bed?"

She smirked. "Have at it. But, you can't talk to me while I'm trying to work."

Okay.

Cool.

I could respect that.

I spent the next couple of hours dozing, messing around on my phone, watching her.

Studying her.

Damn near ethereal in beauty, draped in that same soft robe from the last time. The artificial light cast a bluish radiance over her dark skin, contributing even more to that other-worldly quality, making it easy to wonder if this whole thing – meeting her at all – was some sort of long, fucked-up dream.

An illusion.

My head went to, left, and revisited myriad places and

possibilities between then and when the sun finally started coming up, replacing the illumination from her computer with the muted sheen of daylight through the shades.

I used the room phone to order breakfast when I heard her stomach rumble.

I didn't try to be quiet about it, just looked her dead in the face while I ordered us avocado toast and breakfast potatoes from the onsite restaurant.

"So are you going to answer my question?" I asked her once she'd got some food down.

She met my eyes with a smirk. "Why are you so interested?"

"Why wouldn't I be?" I asked her. "It's the entire basis for how we met. Allegedly."

Shaking her head, she laughed. "Here you go with that again. Why do you think I'm keeping some secret first meeting from you or something?"

"I didn't say all of that," I chuckled. "But... you know..."

"You think I'm a witch or something – *obviously*."

I chuckled. "Your pussy *is* quite hypnotic, so shit... you tell me."

"You sure know all the right things to say to a girl," Hailey grinned, sauntering to where I'd gotten back into bed after breakfast. Her robe pulled open as she sat, and she made no moves to correct it. "I'm quite sure my new neighbors hate my ass. Construction is loud as hell. The restoration company has already pulled up the old foundation and poured the new one. I think framing is next week. It's moving fast."

I nodded. "Yeah, because they have their own contractors. They don't have to wait around for anybody because the contractors for everything are on staff. They stay busy, around this area. A lot of the older stuff is all falling apart. Shoddy construction. Or shoddy remodeling work."

"Yeah, like what happened to me. It's a damn shame."

I grunted. "It's more than a shame – the shit is actively dangerous. We got called yesterday to a duplex that collapsed. Out of nowhere. Multiple families inside, kids. Insulation, wires, bricks... debris *everywhere*. It's precarious, because if you charge in there trying to throw shit out of the way, you make it an even more dangerous situation, for the people you're trying to get to *and* for yourself."

Hailey blew out a breath. "And it was on fire?"

"No, there was no fire. The foundation failed. Had probably been failing a while, and nobody knew. Low-income housing – building owned by somebody in... who the fuck knows? But they've got people in there thinking all is well. Everybody's good, kids doing their homework, somebody getting dinner together, somebody getting ready for work, all these people going about their day. Then suddenly the fucking sky is falling, and there's no ground under your feet anymore."

"That's *awful*. Were you guys able to... was everybody...?"

I shook my head. "Nah. A twelve-year-old, and an eighty-four-year-old. The elder had a heart attack, we couldn't get her to the hospital before she was gone, and couldn't bring her back. And the kid... was in the basement practicing guitar. That would never be a great outcome, but if we could've gotten to him earlier... We couldn't get to him before he couldn't breathe."

It was *always* hard to lose people during a shift.

Alive one minute, gone the next.

But kids?

That was the worst.

"That's why you were in a shitty mood last night?" Hailey asked.

"I was?"

"You said so. You were definitely going through something you took out on my pussy. Not that I'm complaining," she added. "Do you need to talk about it or something?"

"Are you offering?"

Her lips pursed, considering it. "Strangely enough, I think I am?"

"Why is that strange?"

She shifted position, looking at the ceiling instead of at me. "I

interview people. I don't give them a shoulder to cry on —
metaphorically, that is. Usually when people are spilling their beans
to me, it's with some deeper purpose. Gathering information, telling a
story. Never just to get it out."

I chuckled. "So I ask again, is this an offer? Cause you don't seem
enthusiastic."

"I think I'm a little confused."

"About?"

"You. Yes, there's the obvious — tall and handsome, good dick,
but that's never been enough for me. Not for more than a brief good
time."

"Oh, so you're a player?" I asked, prompting her to laugh.

"I wouldn't call it that."

"What would you call it?"

"I'm .. me. I'm Hailey."

I nodded. "Well *Hailey,* to answer your question... there's nothing
to talk about. At some point, you get used to it. Never quite numb,
but you can't let yourself believe it's rare. You go into these
emergency situations knowing, more likely than not, the odds are
completely stacked against you. You've got to be the kind of person
who can say, *fuck the odds*, I'm going to try everything anyway."

"Do you ever get burned out? For lack of better phrasing."

I scoffed. "In this profession, when you're burned out, you *quit.*
You can't be half in, half out when people's lives are on the line. Stay
your ass at home. Somebody depending on you to take their next
breath, and you're not even sure you want to be at work that
day? Nah, it doesn't fit."

"So why do you do it?" she asked, finally bringing her gaze back
to me, then moving until our faces were inches apart. "You like being
the hero or something? Is it an ego thing?"

I shrugged. "*Everybody* wants to get clapped for at their job, so if
that's ego... yeah. I guess so. I enjoy making a difference. I enjoy
saving lives, saving livelihoods. I enjoy fighting against something *that*
powerful and winning. Obviously, that doesn't always work out in

everybody's favor, not the way we might want it to, but... it's one of those things. When it's bad, it is truly *fucked*. But when we can pull out a good result? It's really damn good. The good results keep you going," I explained. "And, fire and rescue is in my blood. I come from a family of firefighters, paramedics, nurses, all that. My father was a firefighter, so that's all I ever saw. All I've ever wanted to be."

"That's really cool," Hailey smiled. "The only thing that runs in *my* family is overbearing mothers. And *that* curse ends with me."

"Damn, a curse?" I laughed. "Is it really that bad?"

"No," she shook her head. "I give her a hard time, but I love my mother. As long as she's where she's at, and I'm where I am, me and her are perfectly good. It's when we're in the same room that things get a little sticky."

"What about your dad? You're giving me smart-mouthed teenager vibes, so I'm wondering if you got along with him."

"Oh, my father was my *bestie*," she laughed. "My mother says I'm just like him, which is probably why she and I have friction. I was very much a daddy's girl."

"Was?"

"Yeah. He passed a few years back. Sickle-cell complications."

"Damn. I'm sorry to hear that."

She gave me a wry smile and nodded. "Yeah, me too. What about you? You get along with your folks? Cause *you* definitely give *me* golden child of the family vibes."

I chuckled about that, because... she wasn't wrong. "I count my parents among the best people I know. My father is a retired fire chief, my mother is a retired pediatric nurse. Served people their whole lives. Passed it down."

"You're an only child?" she asked.

I shook my head. "Technically, no. I was the only child my parents gave birth to, but they were parents to half the neighborhood. Anybody who needed it. And they're grandparents to half the neighborhood now," I chuckled. "Which completely takes any pressure off my back, so I love it."

Hailey laughed. "They sound like lovely people."

"You should meet them," I said, not even thinking about it.

Hell, I didn't even realize really it had happened until Hailey's eyes popped open wide.

"*Not* you inviting me to meet your parents. I know you said the pussy was hypnotic, but *wow*."

I lifted my hands between us. "Believe it or not, I did not even *remotely* mean to say that," I confessed. "I'm not...*we're* not... you know what I'm trying to say."

"I actually *don't*," she claimed, smirking. "Please say more words, and be super specific."

"You play too much," I told her, prompting yet another laugh, confirming that she was indeed playing.

"I'd actually *love* to meet your parents, Ellis," she said after another moment, taking on a completely serious expression. "Like I said, they sound like lovely people, and if they've been around this neighborhood, been part of the fabric of it, I bet they'd be able to give me some historical insight that could be really valuable."

"Valuable for...?"

"My article," she answered, gesturing at the computer. "It's part of what I'm doing here. I was supposed to be rehabilitating the house and digging into the history of my ancestors, the history of Blackwood. Now I'm doing it while we... *rebuild* the house I guess."

"Sounds interesting."

"No, it doesn't," she laughed. "But it'll *be* interesting enough, for people who are into such things. In the meantime, I still have things to do for work — starting with having to find a fresh local interest piece that I can do for the magazine. A local business or something. You got any suggestions?"

"Well, *Night Shift* is going to be opening a new barrel for the first time soon – a brew we've been aging in bourbon barrels for more than a year now. It's time to pop it open, taste it, see what we've done."

Hailey frowned. "We? I could have sworn I asked you when you were telling me about *Night Shift* in the first place if you were connected to the family business."

"I'm *not* connected to the family business," I explained. "The brewery though, I'm all up and through it. I'm part of *that* team," I explained. "Recipe development, process alignment, bottling techniques, timing. It's a hobby of mine."

She raised an eyebrow at me. "The things you named off sound much more intense than a hobby."

"Okay," I shrugged. "Maybe a bit more than a hobby. Maybe more like a passion."

"And that's why you went to *Night Shift* after having a hard day?" she correctly surmised. "Lark told me you were checking on the tanks or something. But it was more than that, right? You were going to your happy place?"

I chuckled. "Something like that. Is that what writing is for you?" I asked her. "Your happy place?"

"Yes and no," she grinned. "Writing is... as rewarding as it is tragic. Cathartic and devastating. Peace and purgatory at the same damn time. I *love* it," she laughed. "There is nothing else in this world I'd rather do."

"Strangely enough, that sounds a lot like being a firefighter," I laughed.

She nodded. "So we have something in common."

"So it seems."

I could converse with her like this all day, all night, into the next. Hell, I *wanted* to.

But I *did* have somewhere to be.

In fact, I was due at the brewery for a meeting about opening the barrel, figuring out our parameters and contingencies, as well as the event surrounding it, all of that. There was planning to be done, and testing, and *more* planning.

I really needed to be at that meeting.

I really didn't want to leave.

"I have to go," I told her anyway, and she nodded.

"I figured. I'm sure we'll run into each other again somewhere along the way," she smiled. And then her expression got very serious. "I booked this room for at least the next month so you know."

I tipped my head. "So what you're saying to me is...?"

"Make sure you keep up with that key."

NINE
HAILEY

I DIDN'T GET NERVOUS.

That wasn't really a *thing* for me.

Whatever else I could say about my mother, her child-rearing philosophy had struck a delicate balance between insanely critical and incredibly encouraging. I had spent most, if not all, of my life believing that anything I wanted to accomplish was within my reach.

If there was something I couldn't do, okay, we were learning how.

Something outside my immediate grasp?

Fine, we could be patient.

Too far to get there in a day?

Cool, we'd take it in steps.

She might nitpick and critique the absolute hell out of me at every step along the way, but she never accepted claims of what I *couldn't do.*

Even the journalism career she inexplicably despised.

So with all this coursing through my veins, I walked into *Sugar&Spice* with absolute confidence that I could excel at the role I was stepping into.

Which made the knot in my stomach even more baffling.

I checked myself in the mirrored wall of the elevator as I headed up to the suite of offices to meet with the editor-in-chief – the HBIC – Cameron Taylor.

I'd worked with Cameron before, and truly enjoyed her—as a person and as a boss. It was part of the reason I'd been looking forward to this and made the twist of uncertainty in my belly even *more* annoying.

I didn't understand why I was feeling so weird about this – it wasn't as if this was anything I hadn't done before.

Isn't it though?

I paused with my hands smoothing the flowy navy-blue pants I'd paired with a simple, gauzy white top. I felt good about my outfit choice – a trip to a few boutiques around town had replenished my wardrobe, putting me back on what more than one person who knew me had referred to as my "Erykah Badu shit". My hair had fully cooperated this morning, my skin had never looked better, and my new perfume had me wanting to take *myself* back to the hotel for some booty.

Getting beyond the physical stuff, I knew I could walk into a room and hold my own in a conversation with anybody. I could weave the hell out of some words. The job was already mine – it wasn't as if this was an interview.

So what the hell was different?

Well, the job was.

I'd spent my entire career as a freelance writer, coming and going as I pleased. I wasn't beholden to any certain publication, and I didn't stand for being pulled into the middle of any kind of rivalry. It didn't matter that you had beef with the magazine I wrote a piece for last month, if you wanted my byline in your shit you came correct, and people did it.

"*That island unto yourself stuff is going to get old after a while.*"

I vividly, *vividly* remembered my father saying something along those lines to me for the first time, and it had been easy for me to brush off for a long while. He never said it the same way, but the sentiment remained the same throughout my life.

If I was lucky enough to meet him again in another timeline, I hoped I remembered to cuss his ass out for that.

Because here I was, boxing myself into the constraints of a "real job", because the alternative had gotten old.

This was new.

It was new as hell.

Mostly, I understood there wasn't too much that would change, especially in terms of my writing. Now though, I would be responsible for *other* writers, would have people looking to me for advice and guidance.

Which was fine.

I got emails from young writers all the time.

It was never an issue for me to give them a little of my time, to share what I knew.

The difference was, I responded to their emails and went on about my day, maybe checking in later, nothing major. I remembered their names, smiled when I saw their bylines come up.

But having people knock on an office door to talk to me?

Having to look them in the face while I gave them critical feedback?

That was another, exotic animal.

I could handle it.

It was just uncharted territory.

A new challenge to conquer.

I walked off the elevator with my head held high, already knowing exactly where I was going. I bypassed the reception desk up front, heading straight to the back office where I knew Cameron's set up was.

As I was heading in, I recognized her husband, Will, on his way out.

Wearing a Blackwood Fire Department uniform. Him being a

firefighter was not new information to me, but the number emblazoned on his uniform still caught me off guard.

Thirty-four.

He works at the same station as Ellis.

We didn't really know each other, so we only exchanged a smile and a nod as a passing greeting, but still – the sudden mental imposition of someone I was trying to get off my mind had me a bit shook as I made my way to Cam's office.

I must not have been as good at hiding it as I thought I was, because the first thing off Cameron's lips as she came out to greet me was, "Are you okay?"

Quickly I nodded, wanting to assure her I would not be *that* girl at the office, who needed to have her artsy-fartsy feelings managed every time she came in the door.

"Yes, I'm completely fine – just feeling very *aware* of everything right now."

Cam smiled. "Understandable. And I mean, who could blame you if you *weren't?*" she added. "Your house burned down within a week of you moving here. It's okay if you're not okay. But since you say you are, I'm going to treat you like you are."

I grinned, returning the hug she offered with a squeeze. "And that is absolutely appreciated," I told her.

"Come on," she said, linking an arm through mine. "Let me show you to your office."

It wasn't very far from her, and certainly not as large.

But still... *damn.*

"This is an office fit for my new executive editor, right?" she asked, gesturing at the beautiful, exposed brick and enormous windows. "I didn't bring anything in, because I assumed you'd want to decorate it yourself. There's a budget set aside for you to do so. Elaine, whose position you're taking, is available to you for consultation for another two weeks before she's off to *Speak, Play, Grub* over in Africa."

"Good," I nodded. "Because you know I've never taken on a position like this before, right?"

"Yes," Cameron laughed. "You've made sure I knew that about three or four different times. Listen, I know you came to me about a staff writer position, but Hailey... It's like putting Beyoncé on a chorus," she laughed. "Yeah, it's a good time and a hot song, but you'd rather have the full experience. I think you've been singing a lot of choruses – it's time to see what you can really do."

I wasn't going to do it, but it *could* be argued that coming in to work for someone else was giving up, or putting a limit on my creativity. What *I* knew, though, was that I'd gone as far as I cared to on my own, and now it was time to pick up a different sort of accolade.

Becoming executive editor at one of the largest Black magazines in the country wasn't playing small by any means.

Yes, I was coming in hot for my first executive level position, but it wasn't as if I hadn't earned it. I'd worked at smaller newspapers, magazines, local news blogs, you name it. I knew the work that went into a publication, and knew what went into my job. I left that world to work on my own before I'd ever climbed up the ranks enough to actually do it.

Now it was time.

"Let's order some lunch," Cameron suggested. "I know you just got here, but we can get some tapas from Honeybee and graze while I go over production schedules, responsibilities, all of that with you."

"First day on the job and I already get to have lunch with the editor-in-chief, I'm honored," I teased her, and she chuckled.

"Only until you're tired of me talking your ear off," she countered. "But don't worry, I have a limit on it, since the captain says I have to be home on time today."

"The captain?" I asked, following her back out of my office and into hers.

"My husband," she explained. "He got promoted to captain at his station, and what started as me teasing him about *that* ended up sticking, and I mess around and call him that in mixed company. Sorry."

"*No*, no need to apologize, at all," I assured her. "It's nice. Do you guys always have dinner together?"

She shook her head. "We rarely do. With his schedule, it's always kind of been a thing of fitting in around each other, and we've always been able to make it work. But he is actually acting fire chief right now, so his schedule is even more all over the place with the extra responsibility. We're having to get it in where we can, hence, *make sure you have that ass waiting for me today*. And guess what I'm going to do?"

"Have that ass waiting, I know that's right," I laughed as we stepped into the office.

I expected nothing less than a good time dealing with Cameron Taylor, because I *always* had a good time with her. Our food arrived, and we spent the rest of the afternoon going over everything I needed to know for the position, down to the names of the staff writers, photographers, illustrators, and anyone else on hand whose work would contribute to the editorial content of the magazine. My position was not to be confused with the creative director, but I had a lot of authority that came along with it. Everything needed to serve the overall mission and vibe of *Sugar&Spice*, which was essentially education, entertainment, and empowerment for the Black community.

I could interpret it as I wanted, and of course work together with the other directors to create a cohesive product.

It was a lot, but I was excited.

That excitement carried me all the way out the door that evening, exhausted and hungry, but certainly looking forward to everything that was coming my way.

Except for a phone call from my mother.

The sound of her distinctive ringtone sent a lightning rod of anxiety down my back. We'd been on a consistent schedule of communication for most of my adult life.

Every three to four days when we were on the best of terms.
Rare.

Every week when we were in a pretty neutral place.
Usual.

At minimum, bi-monthly when we weren't really cool, but also understood the need to at least check in with each other.
Too often.

Today was day seventeen since we last spoke, so I knew I was pushing it.

"Let me guess – you've gotten yourself settled into Blackwood, and already your telephone doesn't work anymore?" was the way she greeted me when I answered the phone.

Unsurprising.

"I've been extremely busy," I answered.

"Busy with?"

"Well, the house, my job, living."

"The job?"

"Yes, Mama the job. I started my position at *Sugar&Spice* today. Remember me telling you about that?"

"Well, you've written for them before, but that's not a job."

"It's definitely a job, and I'm not just writing now. I'm executive editor for the entire magazine. It's a huge position. Which I'll have an assistant for, maybe two."

I wasn't bragging, just trying to get her to understand.

"Fancy. Congratulations," she said, with none of her typical sarcasm, which let me know that she really meant it, which was... strange. "And how is the house coming along?"

I swallowed hard as I continued up the street, with the hotel as my destination. "The house is coming along fine," I said. "I have a phone call with some contractors tomorrow."

It was absolutely the truth, just... without the parts that would start a conversation I didn't want to have.

"You know a lie by omission is still a lie?" she asked.
Shit.

Shit shit shit.

"Who talked?" I asked, stopping to glare down the street as if whoever it was would pop up in front of me.

"*Google*," my mother trilled, and I could practically hear the hum of excitement in her voice. "So you weren't going to tell me you went up there and burned the damn house down?"

"*I* didn't burn anything down," I defended. "It was an accident because of faulty wiring. An investigator came out before they tore it all down."

"Tore it all down. Wow. And how much of your savings did you blow through to waste on that?"

"I didn't blow through anything, the homeowners' insurance is cutting me a check. And besides that, I never touched my savings. I used my inheritance."

She gasped. "Hailey Freeman, are you telling me you used *that man's* money to buy my great-great-grandmother's house?"

"No, I'm telling you I used my *inheritance* on exactly the type of thing my father would have wanted me to do – chasing down my curiosity about *my* great-great-great-grandmother."

"Oh, here you go," she huffed. "Your precious, do-no-wrong Daddy who hung the moon for you supported your dreams while your mother is an overly critical monster."

I smirked. " I'm not sure what you want me to say since that's exactly what happened?"

"So you admit you think he's perfect?"

"Mama, he's dead. And I never said that."

"Well, you may as well have."

I let out a deep sigh. "I literally do not have time for this. Is this why you called?"

"I called to see what you were doing to our ancestral home."

"It sounds like you already knew what was happening with the house."

"Yes, but I wanted to hear it from you. Instead of from the streets, which is what I had to do."

I rolled my eyes. "You googling local news stories from Blackwood is not the *streets*. And maybe if our conversations didn't go like this, I would have been more comfortable simply calling and telling you. Instead, I handled the fact that I woke up in the middle of the night to a house fire, alone. I'm going through the process of rebuilding, alone. Every step of the way, alone."

Well... except for Ellis and his dick.

But it really wasn't the same thing, was it?

"Wait, it happened in the middle of the night?" she asked, her tone suddenly shifting.

"Yes," I snapped. "I had an extinguisher, and I tried to fight it but it was useless."

"Hailey Freeman, you tried to fight a house fire on your own with a fire extinguisher?"

"What else was I supposed to do? I knew this conversation was going to happen eventually, and I was trying to prevent it."

"By risking your life?"

"Yes, by risking my life," I answered. "I would literally rather face death than have this conversation with you, and I still have to do both. *Lucky me*."

"Hailey..."

"I've got to go," I said, shaking my head. "I'll talk to you another time."

I didn't hang up, she did.

As if she was the one with the right to be upset about how the conversation had gone.

She and my grandmother *both* had been completely content to let nothing even happen with the house, to ignore the fact that it was still here. And they wanted to treat me as if I was wrong for trying?

I didn't need that shit.

Instead of dwelling on it – well, *trying* not to dwell on it – I had dinner at Arcadia like usual, and then went up to my room to take the longest, hottest possible shower.

I climbed it into bed, frustrated and exhausted and inexplicably horny as hell. But I wasn't in the mood to go to *Night Shift* trying to hunt down Ellis, who I still hadn't exchanged numbers or any further contact information with. And the thought of getting *myself* off made me even more annoyed, because I knew that would not quite do it.

So I went to sleep pissed off.

I woke up a few hours later to the sound of my shower going.

I hadn't heard him come in, but I knew... it was Ellis. A few minutes later, the shower turned off, and then a few minutes after that, I heard the bathroom door creak open.

A moment after *that*, he joined me in the bed.

Instant comfort and relief swept over me as he wrapped his arms around me from behind, pulling me against him. He said nothing, and neither did I, just sunk into him as his lips came to my neck for a soft peppering of kisses that became gradually more urgent, more fervent.

His dick was hard against my back, impossible to ignore as his kisses turned into long sucks and slow flicks of his tongue. He turned me over onto my back, climbing on top of me and pushing my nightgown up and over my hips. By the time he was sinking to me, those kisses, licks, sucks, had teeth added to the mix. Little nips along my neck and collarbone that he soothed with his tongue as he buried himself in me in languid strokes.

When his lips came to mine, they were bruising and urgent, seeking something I couldn't identify, but was more than willing to give.

I was willing to take too – every thick inch as he sank into me over and over, every dip of his tongue as he explored my mouth, the urgent grip of his hands as he eased them under me to pull me closer, spread my legs to open me wider, pushed my legs up to sink deeper.

He... needed this.

I felt it.

And I did too.

All of it.

The delicious friction as he stretched the depths of my pussy to perfectly fit his dick?

Necessary.

The smoky sweetness of bourbon on his tongue?

Necessary.

The painful urgency of his fingers digging into my flesh?

Necessary.

There was a growl in his tone as he met my gaze in the dark to ask me a question. *"Whose pussy is this?"*

Any other man, I would have laughed in his face.

But Ellis?

My eyes didn't waver as I told him the truth. *"Yours."*

That seemed to make him fuck me harder. Seemed to make him put a little more oomph in his hips as he lowered his body to mine, anchoring me under his weight as he crushed his mouth over mine in a bruising kiss.

He swallowed the euphoric adulations of my orgasm, going on and on until he was pouring into me, and I was swallowing his growls too.

Neither of us moved until it got too uncomfortable to stay as we were.

And even in our walk to the bathroom to complete the usually awkward steps of cleaning ourselves up, there was comfort.

I turned on the shower, and he joined me without hesitation, without seeking permission he didn't need. And then afterwards, when he was using one of the luxurious hotel towels to dry me off, he looked me in the face and asked a different question.

"How was your day?"

My eyes went wide.

Shit.

... I was in trouble.

TEN

ELLIS

"HOW WAS YOUR DAY?"

The simple, innocent enough question seemed to take her off guard as much as it surprised me coming out of my mouth. Not that it was a strange thing to ask—it was almost a reflex these days, with the person on either side of the question having no real investment.

The surprise here was that I *genuinely* cared.

Hailey cleared her throat, then answered. "I started my job today."

"The *Sugar&Spice* position?"

"Yeah."

"How did it go?" I asked, moving on to dry her back.

"I was already acquainted with the editor-in-chief — she and I get along really well, so I'm expecting the best."

"Good. So... what's bothering you then?"

Hailey raised her eyebrows. "What?"

"Yes, you started your job today, but... I feel like there's something else you're not saying. Something not so good."

"Perceptive, are we?" she quipped, stalling before she actually answered. But then she sighed. "I had a not that great phone call with my mother."

"*Not that great*... what does that mean?"

"It means what I said, *not that great*. But there have been much worse. It's not a big deal. I'm used to it, to the point of expecting it."

"Do you think maybe because you're expecting it, you might engage the conversation in a way that contributes to that existing bias?"

She raised a single eyebrow at me this time, before stepping away from the towel I'd been using to dry her off after our shared shower. "No, I don't think that at all. I *know* it, because my therapist already said so. And you see what I've done with that information..."

"Nothing?"

She smirked. "Exactly." She turned, and walked away before pausing—looking good as hell – in the bathroom door. "I'm sorry, how rude of me. How was *yours*? Was it another bad day?"

"What makes you think so?" I questioned with a frown, padding up to where she stood.

She didn't stiffen at all, didn't resist when I wrapped an arm around her waist to pull her against me like it was the most natural thing in the world, because... it kind of was.

"Because you're *here*. I thought that was kind of our understanding. Helping each other work through some of the shittiness of a bad day."

"*Was that* our understanding? Cause I don't remember having that conversation," I told her, meeting her gaze. "To answer your question, I'm here because I wanted to see you. That simple. Is that a bad thing to admit?"

"Bad? No. It's a little..."

"Weird," I filled in for her, chuckling as I slipped my hands over hers to lead her back to the bedroom. "We're going to use your default term."

"Well, I didn't say it, you did," she laughed. "But yes, this little cutesy, intuitive, *I've been waiting for you my whole life* vibe we've got going on is weird. It's established."

My eyebrow shot up. "You've been waiting for me your whole life?"

"I did *not* say that."

"I literally heard it come out of your mouth."

"Those are just the words that I used to articulate my point. You know *exactly* what I'm saying to you, Ellis."

"I actually don't, sweetheart. I want you to make it *very* plain."

Hailey let out a huff as she settled on the bed. "I'm saying that it would *already* be disconcerting to have a vibe like this with someone I just met under *any* circumstances. But what makes it even more egregious is the fact that I don't do *this*."

"You don't have sex?"

She glared at me. "I think we *both* know this is deeper than sex. Even if we haven't talked about it, even if we haven't explored it, it is. And it feels like it's leading to some inexorable destination that contradicts everything I believe about relationships."

"Which is *what*, by the way?" I asked, as I started getting back into my clothes.

"That *I* do not belong in them. During my last attempt, the guy told me I cared more about my career than I did about him. And he wasn't wrong," she admitted. "I had ambition, and nobody was impeding it. He accused me of not loving him. Which wasn't true — I did. But he wanted me to choose the relationship over my career, and I was not in a place for that. I don't know if I'll *ever* be in a place for that. Not that it stopped him from trying again last year. *And a few months ago.*"

She muttered that last part, tacking it on to her statement like an afterthought that made me grin. "Damn Hailey, you got the fellas down bad out here," I chuckled. "Do I need to be scared? Any woman that can make a man come around trying to get that old thang back *thrice*? I feel like I should maybe run in another direction."

"You probably should," Hailey laughed. "But I think you know how that would turn out."

I did.

Even though I didn't know how to explain the innate feeling of rightness when Hailey and I were in the same room that made it hard to not be concerned about my mental health.

Our mental health.

Had we been exposed to something in that fire, some type of weird fumes?

"You're not going to leave me out here vulnerable by myself, are you?" Hailey asked, leaning back onto her elbows on the bed.

A sight that made me wonder why the hell I was putting my clothes on.

"What do you mean?" I replied, not bothering to tear my eyes away from her breasts.

"My eyes are up *here*," she taunted. "And what I mean is, I told you why *I* was single. What about you?"

I shrugged. "For me... I don't know. I hadn't met the right one before. And everything else kind of felt like wasting time. Mine and theirs. It took me a bit to come to that, to realize what it was. Why there was... this plateau I would hit with every relationship I attempted. You don't want to do that to people, you know? Let them believe the relationship might ever be something it really can't. So anybody I've dealt with, I try to clarify that it's casual. And I don't do things that contradict that."

"Things that contradict that?"

"Yeah. Texting all day, being laid up, dropping by the job, shit like that. It all confuses things, so I avoid it. To keep everybody's ego in check, and feelings intact."

"Oh. Is that why you haven't given me your number yet?" she mused.

I sucked my teeth. "Come on, you know what this is. You already have my number, intuitively. You just gotta think about it."

Her lips parted, eyes narrowed in confusion, but she said nothing.

For so long, I could tell she really was thinking about that shit. When her eyebrows dropped into a quizzical look back at me, I tried my best to hold it in, but it only took a few seconds for me to laugh and shake my head.

"Seriously Hailey? I was messing around. Did you *really* think you were going to... what, telepathically know my phone number?"

I dodged as she threw a pillow at me.

"This whole thing is weird," she laughed. "How the hell was I supposed to know?"

"The *moment* you start knowing shit you shouldn't, is the one I'm outta here," I told her. "Nah though, we hadn't exchanged numbers cause honestly? I was trying to play it cool."

"No need to play it cool," she shook her head. "Whatever explosive ending this thing between us is going to have, I'd much rather us get on with it."

"Well, when you put it that way it sounds horrible," I laughed, and she shrugged.

"I don't think I have any exes that don't hate my guts."

"What about ol' boy that came back for the three-peat?"

"A glutton for punishment. That's the only thing I can think of. I'm not *that* great... right?" She asked, stretching even further across the bed, legs open.

"I think we both know *that's* a lie," I said, sauntering over to where she was and stepping between her thighs.

"Then why are you leaving?"

Her fingers made lazy circles between her legs as she met my gaze.

"Because I have to be at my parents' house at the ass crack of dawn to help them with some things. And if I stay over with you tonight, there is zero chance of me having the time or energy to make that happen."

"Sounds like you think I'm a bad influence," she murmured as I dropped to my knees beside the bed. I hooked my arms around her thighs, dragging her to the edge of the bed, putting my face right in line with her pussy.

I never responded to her words, just breathed her in for a moment before I covered her clit with my mouth, knowing she would melt over the sudden onslaught of sensation.

I was not disappointed.

My name burst from her lips as her back arched away from the bed, her hands coming to my head, fingers curling in an attempt to grip my hair. *My* fingers went inside her, stroking and exploring as I lapped her with my tongue.

With a little intentionality, it didn't take long at all before her thighs were vibrating against my head as she came, hard. I gave her a second to catch her breath while I washed my face, then brought back a hot towel for her too.

"Have breakfast with me?" I asked, stopping halfway across the room to pose the question.

She was clearly feeling good, wrapped up under the covers, her eyes half open. "Are you talking about coming back to the hotel before I leave for work?"

"Nah, I can't do anymore of the vegan breakfast shit. I need some bacon or something," I chuckled, shaking my head. "Meet me at Honeybee... let's say ten. If it fits in your schedule."

She looked at me for a long moment before she grinned.

"I'll make it fit."

———

Technology was a gift and a curse.

Especially in the world of craft brewing.

There were things I loved about the way the industry had changed – social media had brought increased visibility and interest, brewing software made it possible to more precisely develop and share recipes, and it was easier than ever to find suppliers for any gear you might need.

Lately, though, these fancy new "brewing systems" that were gaining all kinds of popularity?

Keep that shit far away from me.

That had been my reaction when Laken and the other guys in the BBC – *Brothas Brewing Club* –first brought it up at one of our meetings. They were all as passionate about the process as I was, so I knew it was more to do with curiosity than laziness.

But still.

I understood the appeal of efficiency and control, especially as *Night Shift* expanded into bottling and wider distribution. But I maintained that part of the appeal of *Night Shift* brews was our continued adherence to a more classic way of doing things.

We stirred grains in by hand, tasted them, smelled the hops, watched for a certain amount of bubbles per minute during the fermentation stage. It wasn't about a timer going off on a machine, or what some meter said was the perfect amount of this or that. Sure, we measured and believed in precision, to make sure our brews maintained consistency and all that.

But ultimately, it came down to our senses – the human factor that some fancy brewing machine could never, ever replicate.

I'd been accused before of being a little too into this whole thing.

It was an accusation I was willing to take, but not one I would do anything about.

This shit mattered to me, period.

Which is why I was at my parents' house at five in the morning, helping my father fix fence posts, and replace roof shingles, and figure out why the garage door was so loud, and power wash the driveway.

It was a sacrifice of three or four hours of my time, in exchange for the beautifully blended fruit purees my mother made for our use in the brewery. The wrong formulation could ruin an entire batch, which was not only a waste of time, but was basically flushing money and supplies down the toilet.

She let me pay her for the fruit, but not for the labor, which was a major thorn in my side. Several times a year I tried to push the issue, and several times a year she cussed my ass out. Which is why showing up to help my dad with a honey-do list that was a bit more than he could take on by himself as arthritis and old age slowed them down was about the *least* I could do.

My mother got the stuff she wanted around the house done, my father got the help he needed without having to actually ask for it, and got to pretend my presence was a pain in the ass. I got to spend long, engaged hours with my father, and somewhat repay my mom.

It was a win for everybody.

I wrapped up a little earlier than usual with my parents, and got out of the house with only a few biscuits, some cheesy scrambled eggs, and one slice of ham forced into me. I had enough time to wash up and then head over to *Night Shift* to check in on one of my favorite things.

Brew day.

With these shifts I was on, it was important to maximize my time between. Yes, I needed plenty of rest in order to be productive and alert while I was on the clock, but spending all my hours off work sleeping was the last thing I cared to do. Which was why I'd sought Hailey's presence — *not* because it had been a shitty day, like she thought. I was getting in the time I could. Not that spending a few hours inside her *wasn't* a cure for what may or may not have been ailing me, but I had no interest in using her as simply a vessel for blowing off steam.

I cared more than that.

Which was wild.

"Uh-oh, here he comes!" I heard as soon as I stepped around the corner into the warehouse behind the bar that housed our brewing setup.

I couldn't do anything but laugh at Laken's teasing, since a few days ago, I had sworn up and down that I was *not* neurotic about this process. That I *didn't* have to have my hands on it.

My showing up here now was evidence to the contrary.

It wasn't until I was really down in there with them – them being Laken Kimble, owner of *Night Shift*, and Keith, another part of our brewing team – that they stopped laughing to give me a strange look.

"You stopping by a GQ shoot after this or something, my man?" Laken asked, making me frown.

"What?"

Keith was the one to speak up, answering my question. "Bruh, ain't nobody seen you in jeans and an actual shirt in a long time. These definitely ain't your usual brewing clothes."

I shrugged. "I'm dressed like y'all are normally dressed."

"Yeah, and *we* are dressed like you're normally dressed," Laken countered, gesturing at his sweats and t-shirt — light, comfortable clothes that lent themselves to possibly getting dirty or ruined during some part of our brewing process. "You got a photographer coming out here today or something?"

"No, damn. I can't put on clothes without y'all clocking me?"

"Our bad," Keith laughed, tossing up his hands. "Didn't mean to hit a sore spot."

Laken scoffed. "Nah, fuck that, *I* did. I need to know where your head is at, Boyd."

"My head is fine," I assured with a shrug. "I've got plans soon. I'm just showing my face, peeking in. I'll be back later to check in, in my normal clothes, once I'm done."

"Ooooh! Sounds like a hot morning date to me."

Ah, hell.

That statement came from Keris, Laken's fiancée and *Night Shift*'s creative director.

"Come *on*," I groaned. "I thought we had a bond, Keris, and you doing me like this?" I asked, giving her a hug as she approached us with a folder in her hand.

"I love you like salted caramel cheesecake, Ellis, but I've gotta call it like I see it. Is it that pretty chocolate sister you've left this bar with *twice* now?" she asked, batting her eyelashes.

"*Lark*," I grumbled, shaking my head as the others laughed.

"You know my sister can't hold water when she thinks there's a chance somebody might be in love," Laken reminded me. "She was welcoming Keris to the family a week or two after we met. Almost scared my woman off."

"Um, excuse you – nobody was scaring me off," Keris said as Laken wrapped an arm around her.

"Stop lying in front of folks girl."

For some people, the PDA was embarrassing, but I'd been ten toes down with Laken since he came up here. A good ten years ago, maybe more, I couldn't really remember.

What I could remember was being in a different, shitty bar, and overhearing him talking shit about how every craft beer he tasted, he could "*always tell some white boys had made it*".

Well...we'd fix that.

Between his ancestral knowledge of spirit making and my interest in it as a hobby, our friendship had been born, and like any excellent beer – developed. I'd seen him go through a lot – the loss of his brother, losing several pregnancies, losing his marriage, losing his father.

He bounced back from each of those blows, but over the years I've seen how each one wore on him a little more. Keris coming into the picture had replaced a lot of blown out bulbs.

"Answer the question, Ellis," she said, after she and Laken had exchanged a brief kiss. "If you're dressing up for a woman, I *know* sis is special."

Shit.

I couldn't even bring myself to tell the lie that I didn't know about the "special" part, because I damn well did.

Because she was.

Purely based on inexplicable feelings, not facts.

Even though the facts I knew contributed to the belief.

"Her name is Hailey, and I'm supposed to be meeting her for breakfast in like an hour."

"Hailey ain't got a last name?" Laken asked.

"Damn, *nosy*," I chuckled.

"*Answer the question*," Keris sang. "And when can we meet her?"

"Hailey Freeman," I answered. "And, no time soon, cause I don't want y'all questioning her. Now, can we get started with this brew or not?"

I didn't have time to stick around for much of it, but I took it upon myself to do the milling of the grain that the beer was built around. That took me less than five minutes, and then Keris pulled me aside to show me mockups for this brew's design, based on the things I'd told her about it.

"So I've got two different names I'm thinking, but the design is the same for either," she explained, flipping open the case of the tablet she was carrying – what I'd mistaken as a folder. She turned on the screen, holding it out in my direction. "Since we're riffing off the *Rookie* brew, which is an old favorite, and infusing some new flavors, you talked a lot about familiarity, how it may be almost comforting to the taste buds. So... I'm thinking we go with either *Deja vu*, or *Next Lifetime*," she said, showing me two different versions of the same design, with the different names.

The design was cool as hell, featuring stylized replay symbols, clocks, infinity symbols, and another one that I didn't recognize.

"What's this?"

Keris grinned. "*That* is a Ghanaian symbol — *Yebehyia bio*. Supposedly an adinkra that means, *goodbye, but I'll see you again*. That one might have to come out, because I found that during my internet research and I've still got to do a bit more to make sure that's actually correct, you know. But if it *is* correct, I felt like that was a really cool addition. Especially since the original brew is retiring."

"Yeah, that's cool," I agreed. I gave my preliminary approval on the design since it was a recipe I'd developed on my own, knowing that Laken and Lark would be the ones doing the final approvals. I helped a bit more with the brew day process before I had to move on, heading over to *Honeybee* for my breakfast date with Hailey.

I arrived before she did, which meant I had the pleasure of seeing her walk in, wearing a long, flowy maxi dress that complimented her beautiful dark brown skin, and every one of her curves.

Deja vu.

It hit me then – *that's* what the feeling was, that thing between us I'd been experiencing but couldn't pinpoint. I was confident, though, that we had *not* met before.

So how the hell is the feeling this strong?

Hailey smiled when she spotted me, immediately heading in my direction so we could be shown to a seat.

"Good morning," she hummed, and there was no hesitation in my actions as I pulled her against me and pressed my lips to hers.

"Good morning to you too."

ELEVEN

HAILEY

So Ellis and I were becoming a *thing*.

Which was dangerous.

I was more of the *"thank you for the dick, would you like a piece of gum on your way out?"* kind of chick.

Not the dinner dates, long talks on the phone, *way too early in the morning pillow talk* type.

In the "before times", at least.

Now, there was this pattern developing between the long shifts Ellis worked. He'd come to my room to sleep, then go off to do whatever it was he did – making beer, seeing his parents, hanging with his friends, all that. We had meals together, spent hours indulging each other's sexual whims, cuddled and talked, slept.

And he didn't interrupt while I surrounded myself with those plants to set the perfect vibe to scribble down notes.

He made it effortless to get used to his constant company.

In a *very* short time.

Shit I *did not do*.

Except... I definitely did.

I definitely *was*.

You're thinking about it too hard, I scolded myself – just the push I needed to shake off my qualms and focus. I was supposed to be concentrating on work, and yet my mind kept drifting away.

I pushed it right back though, because I *definitely* had other things that required my focus. Besides the way I'd dived right in with the editorial load at *Sugar&Spice*, I'd finally pulled together my research for my story about *Night Shift*. I wanted to have all the publicly available background information I could before I approached the owner about the angle of my story.

I couldn't chastise other writers about being under-prepared if I was too.

Night Shift itself was less than ten years old, but the owner – Laken Kimble – had deep ancestral roots in the liquor business, thanks to *Kimble Family Bourbon*.

And that wasn't all, either.

Laken's mother – Marlene Broussard by maiden name – was a Louisiana native, and as I dug deeper, I found connection there to other "Freemans". Freeman was a common surname, so it would take digging into some family trees to see if it was the same Freemans as mine. Probably not, but if it was... well, that would be really damned cool.

I had *plenty* to filter through.

If I was going to make this article about *Night Shift* happen, it wouldn't do any good for me to be sitting around thinking about dick.

I closed my eyes, pushing out a sigh as that thought hit me in a strange place.

No, I shouldn't reduce him to his dick, but Ellis and I were clear that I didn't do long-term entanglements. Nor was he looking for anything of the sort.

I didn't know what the expiration date was on whatever *this* was, but there was no doubt in my mind that we had one.

We were going to enjoy it until then.

Focus, Hailey.

Shit.

Okay.

Focus.

"Shit!"

No sooner than I'd decided to *really* buckle down, my phone rang...*hm.*

I was surprised to see the historian, Collette Cole's name on my screen. "Hello?" I answered, anchoring the phone against my ear with my shoulder as I stood from the position I've been in for hours, giving my legs a chance to get a stretch.

"Good morning!" she piped, bubbly as ever. "I am calling because I have some... interesting news for you."

My eyebrow went up. "Really? What's going on?"

"Earlier this week, I was contacted by the granddaughter of your great-grandmother's former neighbor. She recently passed away, and they were going through her things, to see what to divide among the family, what to put into storage, all of that, and they ran across this trunk labeled *Hailey Freeman.*"

"Oh wow," I gushed. "Do you know which Hailey?" I asked.

Obviously it wasn't *me*, but since I was the third in a whole ancestral line of us...

"I'm thinking it was passed down, with your great-grandmother as the last owner before now. The last Freeman to live in the house before the riots," she explained. "Apparently, when the former Miss Freeman fled the city, she left a lot behind. The neighbor – a white woman — went in and gathered up the photo albums and all that for safekeeping. She had been holding on to these things, meaning to get in contact with the family. For whatever reasons that never happened. All of it just stayed in storage. But this granddaughter came across a treasure trove of things she thought might be of some historical value. She got in contact with the city, who put her in touch with me. I asked her to pack it all up and send it to me." She stopped her excited speech to let out a sigh. "Hailey, I think...you may want to come and look at these things."

Not at all an unreasonable request, but something in her tone made me raise my eyebrows.

"Okay, that's no problem, but why did you say it like that?" I asked.

Collette cleared her throat. "I took a peek into the boxes, out of natural curiosity. Some of it is... um... of a very sensitive nature. Things that we wouldn't have been able to display in the museum, even if you'd given us your family's permission."

My eyes went wide. "Sensitive? Sensitive how?"

"Um... of an adult nature."

"*Oh*," I laughed. "What, like some nasty letters or something?" I chuckled. "We all know our ancestors used to get down, that's how we got here. Is that really still taboo these days?"

"Well... it's not *just* the letters."

"So there *are* letters?"

"Yes, there are definitely letters, but there's also... images."

I sat down. "*Images*?! Like nudes?"

"Yes, you could say that."

I rolled my eyes. "I mean come on, they have to be crazy grainy or something like that, right? That would be from like the nineteen-hundreds, photography wasn't *that* advanced."

Collette perked up. "Actually, you would be *quite* surprised at how sophisticated photography was. Of course it's not full HD like what we could do with a camera phone *these days*, but the images are remarkably clear. And... quite explicit."

"Okay. So you want me to come and get my great-Granny's nasty pictures out of your basement. I can do that," I laughed.

"Well... it's not quite *that*," Collette joined me in laughter. "I know how something like this can be sensitive for some families, or maybe even embarrassing. Personally, I think it's fascinating, but I understand *why* this bit of history was buried. My mind is blown by the discovery, and I can't wait to dig further. Think about it — before Playboy was a thing, before Hustler or even the much less explicit ones like... *Jet Beauty of the Week* or whatever else, there was... this."

I frowned. "Whoa, backup," I said, as her words really settled on my mind. "Are you saying that it's not *personal* pictures?"

"Oh! *No,*" Collette answered, amused. "I'm sorry I wasn't clear. Now there are some of what the description says *is* Hailey Freeman, but there's also... others. Men, women, couples and groups of varying genders. Varying expressions of sexuality. It's quite diverse for the time. I don't know that we have a periodical this inclusive *now.*"

"A *periodical?*" I questioned. "I'm sorry, *what?*"

"There is a box full of folded magazines – like *issues* of this, with timely articles, a subscriber list...it's like a whole best kept secret. There *had* to be this agreement, to not talk about it publicly, right? For it to not be widely known. Other people must've destroyed their copies or just don't talk about it."

"That's *insane,*" I said. "A whole damn... I'm... can you snap a picture of a few issues with your cell phone and send it to me or something? I need to see this *right now.*"

"Yes, of course!" she agreed, and we said quick goodbyes with arrangements for me to come through later and pick everything up. A few moments later, my phone pinged with a new notification. And sure enough, there it was.

Lascivious Liberty.

Wow.

Collette didn't open any of them to show me the pictures inside, but the name and suggestive front cover imagery said enough.

This was... *amazing.*

I couldn't wrap my head around how anyone could see it any other way. There were volume numbers, and a different, beautifully illustrated cover on each of the ones in the picture she sent me. *Sense & Sexuality* was the lead story on one, and my eyes watered with tears at the byline *right there* on the cover.

By Hailey Freeman.

Before I could talk myself out of it, I was dialing my mother's number. She answered it like she was annoyed that I was calling, but I wasn't in the mood for that energy with her, nor did I care.

"*Lascivious Liberty*," I spoke those two words, with unexpected emotion choking my voice. For a long moment, neither of us said a word, and really... that told it all.

She didn't ask what it was.

Because she already knew.

"How did you hear that name?" She asked, after it was clear I wouldn't be the one to break the silence, to give her any hint at potential talking points.

Nope.

This was all on her.

"Did you *really* think it would turn out any different from this Mama?" I asked. "I got distracted with the fire, and starting this job, but you *had* to know I would find this. My daddy didn't call me kitty for nothing."

"Oh, here you go with your damn daddy—"

"*Yes*, here I go, cause my *damn daddy,* as you call him, hid none of my family history from me, even when it wasn't pretty! Seriously, Mama? Are you going to finally fess up and tell me what in the world this is all about?"

"*Fess up?*" She asked. "As if you're the parent and *I'm* the child? I know you don't think I owe you some type of explanation, little girl."

I sucked my teeth. "We're both good and grown, and you *do* owe me some sort of explanation. Why in the world you would not tell your *journalist daughter* that her great-grandmother ran a whole provocative, *groundbreaking* publication in the nineteen-freaking-hundreds?! When I wanted to become a journalist, you and Granny acted like I was breaking the family bylaws or something. As if it was *unheard of.* Everybody wants to know your family legacy at BSU, and you made sure I had a story to tell, but it was *so incomplete.* Y'all have sold this whole brand identity around Hailey Freeman being a *seamstress!*"

"Because she was!" my mother snapped at me. "At first. The first Hailey's sewing business built the house, and things were good, and then...your great grandmother took the family name in a different direction. Thank *God* that was left behind when she fled. She started sewing again, started the bridal shop – gave the family a chance to bring back our morals."

"Morals?!" My face dipped into the deepest frown. "Mama, you're kidding, right? There's a reason damn near every woman in our family's last name is *still* Freeman, so I think we're getting a little loose with the judgment."

She huffed. "That's exactly the point, Hailey! We needed to move beyond the generational curses – I don't thank my brother for much, but at least *his* kids are getting married and doing things the right way. Breaking the cycle!"

"Breaking the—no, you know what?" I forced myself to take a breath. "I'm going to act like you didn't even say that to me. Let's get back to you and Granny thinking pretending the magazine never happened was the answer?"

"No one is pretending. We chose not to focus on it."

"*Semantics.* Instead of telling me, *Hailey we don't want you to go to Blackwood digging into your maternal history because we're embarrassed that your great-grandmother was an OG smut dealer,* you treated me like I was stupid for my curiosity. Great."

"If you'd left it alone like we asked, it wouldn't be a problem. But you never listen. Nobody can tell you anything."

My mouth fell open. "And *where the hell do you think I got it from?!* You are literally *the* most stubborn, can't-nobody-tell-me-nothing ass woman I know."

She snorted, exasperated. "And *you* were supposed to be different. Your great-grandmother died when I was very young, but I thought keeping the family tradition of naming you after her would be a chance to right the balance, among other things. I see thinking I was going to restore some honor to the family name was a mistake."

"The *mistake* was thinking honor needed to be restored in the first place," I countered. "Sex and sexuality are not things to be ashamed of."

"Whoring for the entire world to see isn't to be cheered either."

"That's *not* what daddy said you were on back at BSU."

I knew it was a low blow.

Yes.

I did.

So?

"Excuse me?" she snapped.

"I know all about you being *number one hot girl* back at BSU, in your booty shorts, with your fro, getting high, turning my daddy out—"

"*He* corrupted *me!*" she shrieked on the other end of the phone, after a gasp so loud I hoped I hadn't messed around and caused her a damn heart attack.

But honestly, something had to give.

She was being *very* high and mighty about this whole thing, as if she hadn't been shaking ass in the seventies at college. Which is how I ended up fathered by my hippie artist Daddy.

"That's *not* how he told the story."

"Well... I... *We're not talking about me right now!*"

I scoffed. "Of course. We're *never* talking about you, it's always about where somebody else screwed up. You really had me believing my desire to be a journalist was out of nowhere, when it was in my *blood*. And now I'm wondering if my love of nude art wasn't just me being a creep – that was ancestral too."

"It's *vulgar*."

"It's *human*," I countered, shaking my head.

"I hope you're not planning to include this in your little... article. It's private family business, and wouldn't be good for the brand."

My eyes narrowed. "I am *absolutely* writing about it. I am researching, and archiving, and making it all available for public viewing," I told her, *still* shaking my head. "You didn't truly think there was another option for me, right?"

"Hailey, think of the scrutiny – the *shame* this would bring me and your grandmother, and more importantly – the *Freeman Bridal* brand. Think of the stain on your great-grandmother's legacy, after she worked hard to scrub it out, because she saw the light," my mother begged, making me frown.

"I somehow doubt she would see it that way," I answered. "And... wow, I just thought about you asking if *Mama Hailey* would've approve of my coochie-cutters. Turns out, she *really* would."

"Do *not* do this to me!"

"And there we have it – that's the *actual concern*, isn't it?" I chuckled, dryly. "What, are you worried about what the bible study ladies will think about you? Granny?"

"Yes. Exactly."

"*Fuck them.*"

Another gasp.

"Hailey!"

"Look, I don't know why my great-grandmother didn't continue her magazine when she left Sugarleaf," I said. "She probably wrote about it somewhere, but of course you and Granny destroyed it, and of course you wouldn't tell me the truth. So I'll never know," I shrugged. "What I *do* have, no thanks to you, is a connection, *finally*, to someone who doesn't make me feel like my presence in this family is some sort of outlier. Whether you or Granny like it – I'm going to find the story. And I'm going to tell it."

"Hail—"

I didn't wait to hear whatever other bullshit she had to say.

It didn't matter.

I hung up, then got up to find my shoes, so I could go see Collette. I had some history to dig through.

My phone chimed again, and I glanced at it, half-expecting it to be my mother.

It wasn't.

It was Angela, from the restoration company.

Shit.

I'd forgotten I was supposed to be meeting her today, even though it was the whole reason I wasn't in the office. It didn't take much to put my schedule back on track – the collection storage for the museum, where I was meeting Collette, wasn't far from the house.

The house…

The house was interesting before, but *now*?

Had any of the magazine pictures been taken there?

Was there a secret printing press back then?

Had Hailey the second been specifically targeted in the riots because of this, and that's why she ran?

Was *that* why she never went back?

All those questions were turning over in my mind as I approached Angela at the house, which was looking markedly different from what it had been the night of the fire. There were no walls yet, but the framing was in full swing, with roofers starting their work the next day.

"I was *not* expecting it to go this fast," I told Angela, after she'd walked me through the maze of unfinished walls, with the blueprints in hand. "But I'm certainly glad to see it."

"Yes, we pride ourselves on quality work that's efficient. And I won't front – the fact that you could put the money in escrow instead of a loan… we're giving you a bit of priority here, since that's fewer fees and higher margins for *everybody*," she admitted, making me laugh.

"Hey, whatever it takes," I said. "You guys were definitely highly recommended – I'm seeing more and more why Ellis insisted I call you. I'll have to let him know he was spot on."

Her expression shifted to… *something*. "Oh… you know Ellis like that?"

… *okay.*

Eyebrow raised, I said, "I don't know what *like that* means, but he was one of the firefighters the night this all happened. He told me who to call to put it back together."

She dropped her gaze, blowing out a sigh as she shook her head. She was good and grown, but in that moment, she was giving off energy like an embarrassed teenager, contradicting the beautiful maturity of her looks. "Right. Of course. I'm... I'm sorry. I'm being weird."

"It happens," I shrugged, still not sure what the hell was happening. "Seems like he's a sore spot for you or something?"

I was fishing.

Yes.

But I was also right.

Angela sighed again. "Yes and no? We... dated, I guess you could say, about a year ago. I thought there was something there. Like... *really* something. But then he let me know he wasn't really feeling it, so he didn't want to "waste my time". You know – the shit men say and then six months later they're married."

"He's married?!"

Her eyes got big. "What?! No! I mean, not that I know of," she said. "I meant in general. As far as I can tell, he hasn't been serious with anybody since then, but... you've seen him out of uniform, right?"

"I have."

"So you feel me then – a man like that, at our age? What the hell does he mean, *wasting my time?* What time?! We're damn near out of it," she laughed. "So I'm thinking... okay, maybe it's just me, but then he stays single. Although, I *have* heard he's been seen with the same woman a few times. When you brought him up, my first thought was maybe it was *you*, but you said you don't know him like that, so—"

I shook my head, holding up a hand. "I didn't, actually."

She stopped speaking, eyes wide. "What?"

Cringing, I clarified that, "I *didn't* say I didn't know him *like that,* I said I didn't know what *like that* meant," I explained, feeling awkward as hell. "But now that I *do* know what it means... I definitely know him *like that.*"

"Oh. *Oh,* shit," she breathed, then pressed her lips together. "Well. Um... this isn't uncomfortable at all, is it?"

"This is frankly the most relaxed I've ever been in my life," I replied with a little laugh, playing along to keep it from getting any weirder than it already was.

"Glad to be in good company," Angela responded. "Uh... I'm going to get back to the office now."

"Right. Same here," I told her. "We're good though, right? Like, there won't be any weirdness with the house, or—"

"Oh God, *no*! Absolutely not," she assured. "This business is my pride and joy, and I would never jeopardize it over some emotionally unavailable man – no matter how fine he is. Shit. That sounded like shade, and I promise it wasn't—"

"I get it, trust me," I told her, shaking my head. "If you say we're good, I believe you."

"Okay," she nodded. "So... I'll see you for another check-in next week?"

"Yep."

I couldn't get away from there fast enough – and with *new* questions swimming in my already-overloaded mind. I needed to get to my meeting with Collette, so I had to push this new information to the side. Ellis was at work, so it wasn't like I could bring it up with him now.

But the first thing out of my mouth when we spoke again was going to be a very pertinent question.

Have you lost your damn mind?

TWELVE

ELLIS

HAILEY WAS ON SOME BULLSHIT.

I knew from the way she replied to my request that instead of me going to her, she came to me. Through the entire couple months we'd been carrying out this little romance, most of our time had been spent in *her* space, with us occasionally venturing out to share a meal. What had yet to happen was having her in *my* space, and more and more I'd been feeling like that needed to change.

I thought seeing her for the first time after a long shift would be the perfect timing for something like that. Throughout my workday, I wrote and rewrote, edited and revised the invitation in my head. I wanted it to be one she couldn't refuse, so I came up with some extra sauce on it, all of that.

"I need you to grace my home with your presence tomorrow tonight, gorgeous. Good food, good liquor... and whatever else we decide to consume. Let's make it a date..."

Her response?

"Okay."

Damn.

Just... *okay?*

I didn't sweat though, overriding my sense that something was up between us with optimism.

I didn't check in with her when I got off, because I wanted to prepare – I got a good night's rest, made sure my place was spotless, got groceries to cook for her. And then, at exactly the time I'd asked her to arrive, the doorbell rang.

I opened it to find her looking good as hell, like always.

A dress that molded to every curve. Lush natural hair framing her pretty ass face. Sultry deep red on her lips... which were twisted in annoyance, wearing an expression that confirmed the hunch I'd ignored.

"Why the *hell* would you refer me to somebody you've been sleeping with?" she asked, eyebrow raised.

Damn.

Damn, *damn*, damn!

I knew I couldn't avoid this forever, but still.

Damn.

I stepped back from the door to let her in, my mind reeling with how I was going to explain. The truth was the truth, and that was going to have to be good enough because I wasn't about to lie. But there had to be a way to present that truth so it didn't seem so... foolish.

"I don't do games," Hailey said, rounding on me, hand propped on her hip. "Games, drama, competition, none of that. Do you know, part of me wanted to show up here and pretend my little conversation with your old girlfriend never happened? Because bringing it up might turn you off, or might make me look insecure, or whatever other reasons a lot of women would use for burying their feelings for the sake of keeping it cute for a man," she said, in a deathly calm tone that made me a little uneasy.

Especially when her slight sneer shifted to a smirk.

"I'm not a lot of women though – I'm Hailey. And I don't tolerate shit I don't like in general, but for *damn sure* not from a man. And what I don't like *here*, is being sucker-punched with information I should have known. I should have known the man I'm sleeping with used to sleep with the woman who has hundreds of thousands of dollars of *my* money at her fingertips. And *she* is still in her feelings about it. So what's up?"

Oh, she's mad *mad*, I thought, but somehow still couldn't help trying to play it off.

"Well, damn... you said a mouthful," I chuckled, pushing my hands into my pockets.

"Don't I always?" Hailey countered.

I nodded. "True. But, since we skipped the pleasantries, let's backtrack – good evening to you too," I said. "I'm doing fine and yourself?"

"Oh cut the bullshit Ellis," she snapped. "I am *so far* from in the mood."

"Back at you, sweetheart," I scoffed. "I invited you over here for *dinner*, not whatever the hell this is."

Her nostrils flared as she countered, "*This* is me making it plain that I have no interest in being used to play with somebody's emotions. So if *this* is a ploy for you to get that girl to come running back to you or something, you gotta find another bitch for that."

"Is that really what you think of me?" I frowned.

"Have you given me a reason *not to*?" she nipped back. "All the information I have about the situation is that *you* had me putting my money and property in the hands of a woman who is still caught up on you, without giving me any type of heads up about it. So what *should* I think?"

I groaned. "What was I supposed to say?! *Hey, you should know there's a woman walking around Blackwood who might still like me?* Cause let me tell you now—she's probably not the only one."

Hailey's head reeled back, and she let out a laugh that wasn't the kind you used when something was even remotely funny. "This is why I don't fool with you motherfuckers, because you know very well it's not that simple. And the fact that you're acting like it is? Is *really* pissing me off," she contested, neck moving. "She's not just some woman walking around Blackwood, she's someone who I'm paying for a service! I don't like people playing with my time, I don't like people playing with my money, and you have put me in a situation where a clearly emotional woman has control over both. Do not stand in my face and act like its nothing."

With that, Hailey crossed her arms, angry as hell, staring me right in the face and daring me to offer some counterpoint to her words.

Not that I could.

I *hated* drama like this, wasn't interested in any type of yelling or arguing, or any of that —which actually factored heavily into why I *had said nothing* about Angela. I didn't want to create a problem where there wasn't one.

Clearly I'd made a miscalculation.

Usually in a situation like this, the woman ended up backing off, or getting emotional, and then the conversation shifted into managing that.

Not with Hailey though.

I got the distinct feeling that Hailey was more likely to throw hands than throw in the towel, and... I couldn't front.

It was more than a bit of a turn on.

Not that my head should be there right now.

"You're right," I admitted. "It's *not* nothing, and I should have told you. But, I recommended Angela's company to you before anything happened between us. It's an excellent company. I didn't want to bring it up afterwards for exactly this reason. I had no clue if it would ever even come up between the two of you, so what would have been the point of me putting that idea in your head?"

Hailey let out an exasperated huff. "The point would have been giving me a heads up so I'm not blindsided. I get it —you're for the streets, nobody is surprised by that. I mean come on, Ellis, who *wouldn't* have guessed that a tall, broad-shouldered chocolate firefighter with a big dick has left a few women around town frustrated?" she said. "Nobody is asking for, or expecting your damn hit list, but you could and *should* have told me that the woman working on my damn house was on it. Especially as much as you've asked to stay updated on it. You *knew* that woman might be on some weirdo shit."

I pushed out a sigh.

Yeah.

I did.

I did not *expect* her to, but I knew it was a possibility. "I was trying, in my own way, to keep an eye out, so if you told me about any red flags, *then* I could say *maybe it's because of this*."

Hailey rolled her eyes. "Yeah, and in the meantime, this woman looking wide-eyed at me talking about *I didn't know you knew Ellis like that*," she mocked, crossing her arms again. "I don't like that shit. And I can't even play it off in the moment cause I'm caught off guard. It's too much. *This* is too much."

My eyes went wide at that. "Wait, what?" I asked, closing the distance between us. "What are you saying?"

"I'm saying maybe this is enough," she snapped. "Maybe we need to let this go right here, because I'm not—"

"Hey," I stopped her, grabbing her wrists to pull her defiant stance apart. "I know I fucked up by not telling you about Angela. But ain't no *letting us go right here* or whatever this is you're talking about right now."

"Excuse me?"

"You're excused," I chuckled. "It was a breakdown in communication, and I assure you it will not happen again."

Hailey scoffed. "Yeah, I know, because I don't do breakdowns in communication for *flings*. We agreed—this is not some long-term thing."

"Who agreed to that? I agreed to that?"

"I'm not a relationship kind of girl, Ellis. And clearly you're not that guy."

"Clearly?"

"Yeah," she smirked. "Did you not tell ol' girl you didn't want to *waste her time*?"

I frowned. "What does that have to do with you?" I asked, looking her dead in the face. "You're making a lot of assumptions here, Hailey, and if we're talking about stuff the other doesn't like, or doesn't want to tolerate, however you want to phrase it —let's go there. Angela is a wonderful woman – *beautiful* woman. Successful, smart, funny, total package," I admitted. "For somebody else. She was not *my* future, and I knew that, I *felt that*. So I did us both a favor, and instead of "making it work", or hanging in there, marrying her, having kids with her, when I *knew* I wasn't feeling it? I ended it. In order to avoid wasting fifteen or twenty years of both of our lives to end up divorced. I've seen the shit happen too many times. I didn't want that for myself, and I didn't want to do it to her."

Hailey shook her head. "Ellis, you do *not* have to explain—"

"Nah, cause it seems like I do," I spoke up. "Have there been other women since Angela? Yes. Some I wanted to be serious about, some I didn't. But when my gut told me it was time to move on, I did, and I led nobody on, or told any lies along the way. I don't know what your conversation with Angela entailed. I don't know what conclusions you've drawn from it. But one thing I know for *damn sure*, is that me and you? *This* is different. And I've been waiting too long for this feeling to let it slip out of my grasp over a fuck-up on my part."

"And what about what *I'm* feeling?" Hailey disputed, eyebrows raised. "What if *I'm* not feeling it, and don't want to waste *your* time?"

I scoffed. "Woman, look me in the face and tell me that's what you actually believe."

She stared at me until her expression shifted to a glare, nostrils flared, but she could *not* say that shit to me.

Because it would have been a lie.

"I fucked up," I said. "From not telling you about it in the first place, and then not responding well when you confronted it. I can admit that. I should have done better, and I'm sorry that I didn't," I told her, slipping my arms around her waist to pull her into me. "Tell me if there's something I can do beyond my words to make up for it."

At first, she kept right on glaring, without looking in my direction, but then I put a hand under her chin, tipping her face towards mine.

She rolled her eyes. "I don't like this."

"What don't you like?"

"I want to be mad at you. But I'm not. And it's pissing me off."

"So... you telling me you're mad at me for not being mad at me?" I grinned, dipping my head to kiss the velvet soft skin along her collarbone.

"I sure the hell am," she breathed, but with none of the bite her tone had held a moment before. Surely it was hard to sound mad with my lips, teeth, and tongue taking full advantage of the erogenous zone there.

"Why stay mad when I could make you very, *very* happy?" I asked, easing a hand under her dress to slide between her legs, skirting the soft fabric of her panties. "*Goddamn*," I grunted against her neck. She was already soaking wet, making it easy and appealing to slip my fingers into her. "Don't be mad."

"Don't tell me what to do," she whimpered. "I wanna be mad."

"Or do you want my face in your pussy?" I questioned, pushing a thumb against her clit.

"I want to be mad, with your face in my pussy."

So be it.

I backed her up to the stairs that led up to the second level of my loft, not bothering to go all the way up. I spread her open right there on the stairs, yanking her panties aside to dive face-first into the glory between her thighs.

She accepted every point of apology my tongue offered, answering my orally asserted pleas with deep, throaty moans and whimpers. I didn't leave it there either — I made sure she understood I was *extra* apologetic, not stopping my feast between her legs until she was too completely spent to pull herself up from her position on the stairs.

Dress hiked up around her hips.

Legs wide.

Head laid back, arms spread out on either side of her.

But *not* too weak to demand some dick.

I apologized with that, too.

Much later, after our meal, once we were settled on the couch with a couple of beers, she stopped drinking to glare at me.

"What?" I asked, concerned. "I thought we were good."

"Yeah, until I remembered why I was *extra* mad at you," she explained.

"Damn, what else did I do?" I asked.

She rolled her eyes. "*So much* happened yesterday, and I couldn't even talk to you about any of it. Because amid all that other stuff, I get a bomb dropped on me about *you*, too. You and your dick are supposed to be a safe place," she laughed, and I shook my head.

"My bad. You want to tell me what was going on though?"

She blew out a sigh. "I got into it pretty bad with my mother." The humor left her voice as she made that revelation, then took a long sip from her beer.

"Worse than usual?"

"Yeah," she agreed. "Worse than usual. I just don't *get* her, at all."

"What happened?"

"I got a call from Collette – you know, the historian from the museum. You weren't fucking her too, were you?" Hailey asked, making me laugh.

"No, Collette is married to one of my cousins, making her family, damn."

"Shit, just asking," she said. "Anyway, she calls to let me know she's gotten ahold of this collection of artifacts from my great grandmother. Okay wait— let me explain so it's not confusing— *I'm* not the first Hailey Freeman. I'm the third, basically. My great-great-great grandmother who escaped slavery came north, and settled here in Blackwood *before* it was Blackwood. When it was SugarLeaf."

I nodded. "Yeah, I'm familiar with that part of the city's history and all of that. I have people who were here back in those days too."

"Good, so I don't have to explain about the riots and all that. Anyway, so there was a Hailey Freeman. She had children. And her children had children. She passed away, the next girl to be born named Hailey in her honor. Another two generations go on and the same thing happens – when Hailey Freeman passes away, we get a new Hailey Freeman – me. So my great-great-great grandmother is Hailey Freeman. And my great-grandmother is Hailey freeman. And I am Hailey Freeman. This is just to set the stage, okay?"

"Yeah, I'm with you."

"Great. So Hailey the *second* is who these artifacts are from. One thing within this bundle of stuff is this magazine. A magazine from the early nineteen hundreds that is this mixture of... I don't even know how to describe it. Think *Sugar&Spice* magazine pared down to a few articles, and then lots of sexy pictures."

My eyebrows shot up. "Sexy pictures?"

"Yes, *erotic* pictures," she explained, her mouth spreading into a grin. "I still haven't been through everything, but the magazine is called Lascivious Liberty, and it has these articles so far beyond their time. Articles that would still be relevant *now*, about sexuality, and faith, and race, and love, and it's...mind-blowing, honestly. Legitimately *mind-blowing*. This part of our family history, this...this *legacy* of ours should have been carried on, or at the very least *celebrated*. But it wasn't. And I don't understand. The existence of this magazine makes me feel more seen, more at home in my family than I ever have. And come to find out, it's something that my grandmother and my mother are ashamed of. So they kept it from me," she said, her demeanor shifting again before she continued.

"As a teenager, and a young woman, I've been fascinated by the human body, by the ways that we relate to each other. By intimacy. But it was always kind of hammered into me to be ashamed of those things. So I kind of... it's not necessarily that I lost interest, but I kind of dropped the pursuit of it, you know? But being a writer – the journalism, the telling of stories... they couldn't shame that one out of me. I went to school, and I did what I wanted to do, and became who I wanted to be. But it was always with such opposition from them, as if I was bucking tradition or something. And back then, I thought I understood, because we had a family business. When really? I was *living up to it* more than anything. It's ... I don't know," she sighed. "I understand everybody has different relationships with sexuality, and that especially for the generations before us, it's this very complicated thing. But they knew I was coming here, knew I was coming to the house — they *had* to know this was going to come out. Would it really have been so difficult, so shameful, to just... *tell me?*"

Damn.

I really didn't even know what to say about that.

I did, however, know enough to know that the beers we were drinking weren't strong enough for whatever it was Hailey was feeling. So I wordlessly pulled the forgotten bottle from her hand and made it a quick mission to replace with a couple fingers of bourbon.

Much better.

"I think a lot of us have complicated relationships with the past," I said, once I was settled beside her again. "And I think that's especially true for older folks. We're living in a time when it's more acceptable than ever to just...be. Whatever you want to be, being yourself, you can do that. You might get some push back, but more than likely than not, you're going to find community. But our parents' generation, it wasn't as easy for them. And then our grandparents' generation, that was even harder. And this is not to make excuses for them at all," I clarified, even though from the look on her face, it didn't seem like she was offended at all about what I was saying.

She was listening.

"But I think that if it was something that was a secret, at some point it probably became easier to keep being quiet about it than possibly telling a hard truth."

Hailey sucked her teeth. "Are you talking about *them*, or talking about *you*, Mr. *I don't understand what the big deal is?*"

I chuckled, shaking my head. "Nah, I'm not even trying to defend myself on that. I was on some bullshit. And I appreciate that you didn't back off."

"Yeah, that is not even in my nature. I've never been the type to let something that was bothering me go unsaid. And I don't mean like every minor annoyance or anything like that, but big things. Things that could hurt me, or things that could have healed me," she added, with a little sigh. "And I guess that's part of it too, my issue with my mother. Like who is *really* being protected? The brand? What is it you think is going to happen, what do you think people are going to say, and why do you think any of that weighs more than helping your daughter not feel alone? Do you know the battery the knowledge of something like this would have put in my back as a teenager, or as a young woman?"

"It's probably what they were afraid of," I shrugged. "That you'd get a hold of it, and bring it all back. This thing that they've been trying so hard to run away from."

"Yeah," she nodded. "I think you're probably right. I still have a lot to dig through, a lot to read up on and all that, but I wish I could talk to her, you know? To hear from *her* mouth why she left Blackwood, why she never came back, why she didn't revive the magazine, why she let it die like that."

"Did she keep journals or anything? Write letters to people, any of that?"

"I haven't even really gone through a quarter of the box yet," Hailey admitted. "Maybe there's some in there? But I would have loved to hear it directly from her, you know? I want to ask my grandmother if there're stories she knew, things she could pass down, but I know that would be a waste. All they wanna talk about is wedding dresses."

"Wedding dresses?" I asked.

She nodded. "That's what Hailey the second got into after she left of SugarLeaf. She went out west, and I guess decided to not go back into writing or anything. I don't know... maybe there wasn't an industry for it out there. But she knew how to sew – it ran in the family. So, she opened a tailoring shop, like Hailey the first did. Most of her business came from brides, so eventually she started focusing on that, and then... *Freeman Brides* became a thing. I never got to meet her, but I've seen pictures of her in her shop dressing these women for their beautiful days, and I could tell she really loved it. But, she never got married. Which was a little scandalous, honestly."

"Whoa," I chuckled. "How is it a scandal?"

"Um, because *I'm* here, but she was never married. You've got to remember this was the nineteen hundreds. I'm still a Freeman because Hailey the second never got married, but she had kids. And my grandmother never got married, but she had kids. My mother was never married, but she had me. So we're all Freemans. The first Hailey Freeman lost her husband to a devil-ass slaver. So when she came north with her children, she took on Freeman, because she *was*. Hailey the second's father was, um... already married to someone else, so that was a *forreal* scandal," Hailey explained.

"Man, that is interesting. I thought usually the kids ended up with the father's last name, even in situations where the parents aren't married?" I asked.

"Nope, not over here," Hailey said. "It's quite *feminist* if you ask me, but my mother and grandmother would both die over the suggestion."

"Yeah, that tracks," I laughed. "So..."

When I never finished saying anything, Hailey raised an eyebrow. "So...?"

"So, do you feel better now that you've talked through it some?" I asked, reaching over to run a hand along her leg.

She dropped her hand to cover mine, giving it a light squeeze. "You know... yes, actually. Thank you."

"You ain't gotta thank me, all I did was sit here," I shrugged.

"I think maybe that's all I needed," she said. "I rarely vent like this to people. Everybody has their own shit to deal with, without me involving them with mine."

"I don't feel burdened at all," I assured her. "In fact, I'm more than happy to help lighten your load when you need that."

"I appreciate that," she nodded. "I'm *really* not used to that."

"Things change all the time," I offered, and she smirked.

"Of course they do, it's just... this is so different. I came over here fully prepared to get one last teaspoon or two of dick, and then never fucking talk to you again," she admitted. "And now I'm laying my heart out over a glass of bourbon? What even is this?"

"Serendipity," I offered, and she frowned at me, taking another sip from her glass.

"You sound like my father. Are you one of those *everything ends up the way it's supposed to be, no matter what* people?"

"I didn't used to be. Not that I *didn't believe* in spirits and signs and all of that, I just... didn't really think about it. But then my homeboy –Laken, from *Night Shift* – he went through this whole thing with his lady that he's with now. His people are from Louisiana, so dream interpretations, kismet, stuff like that, that's nothing to them. And I'm comfortable telling you this cause he'll tell anybody the story, but his deceased brother actually came to him in a dream, and told him when he was about to meet the love of his life, Keris. Of course, it's easy to say that could have been anybody, but the way it all lined up... it's hard *not* to believe it was preordained by God. Like that is who he was put on the earth for, and when it was time for it all to fall into place, everything lined up. Like they *needed* each other, completed each other. You know?" I asked, and Hailey nodded, fully enthralled with my words. "The day we barreled a brew — first time we ever did that – he proposed to Keris. And they're not really making a big deal about it, kinda making it all about opening the barrel publicly, but... that's going to be their wedding day. There's a bunch of significance around all of that too, but... I won't bore you with all of those details."

"No, *please*," Hailey grinned. "I *love* stuff like this, and I'm definitely going to want to hear all about it for the story... which I still have not pitched to my subjects."

"I thought you were been supposed to start on that?"

"Well, I *was*, but I wanted to have all my stuff together, and now you've introduced this whole additional element for me. I wonder if they'd be willing to talk about it for the magazine," she said, propping her hand on her chin.

"No time like the present to find out," I offered, pulling myself up from where we'd been sitting and extending my hand.

"Seriously?" she asked. "You want to go to *Night Shift*... right now?"

I shrugged. "Why not? Let them tell their own story."

THIRTEEN

HAILEY

THE PICTURES WERE ABSOLUTELY *SCANDALOUS*.

There was really no getting around that.

Lascivious Liberty would be amazing as some sort of archival social media account, with details and back stories and all that. These people that were in the pictures though, there was *no way* I'd ever be able to put these materials somewhere online without going through some sort of legal process to gain permission and photo releases. And how many of their descendants were going to give permission to see their great-grandmothers and fathers, great aunts and uncles, family friends portrayed like this?

Likely very few.

It was a shame.

Because yes, they were scandalous, and some of them were downright vulgar. But more than that, even the vulgar ones were *remarkable*. The eroticism, unfettered sensuality, the candor of it all.

It was delightful.

Some people would find it strange, would have no desire to see their people in pictures like this, but personally... I was *especially* fascinated by the pictures of Hailey the second.

She looked like *me*.

It was uncanny, because I'd always thought I looked more like my father, but those were undoubtedly the same eyes, same lips. Even our bodies were quite similar – a mostly slim build, with a lil something to hold on to here and there.

That was another thing I loved, not just about the pictures of Hailey, but *all* the pictures.

There was no preference given to any certain look— these were people with real, natural bodies whatever that entailed, with what I wouldn't even describe as imperfections.

Just...*realities*.

Soft bellies, rolls, cellulite, sloped asses, stretch marks, sagging breasts, small dicks, and then the opposite of all those, and everything between. It was refreshing, because the magazine wasn't centered on some fantasy from one person's imagination of what perfection looked like.

It was just *real*.

It wasn't just sexy, it was legitimately *interesting*.

Was it just a difference in the times?

A hundred years ago, bodily ideals were definitely not the same as now, and people's relationship with those ideals had to be markedly different back then. In some ways, it felt like in that area, we were frankly freer back then than now.

One of several things that made me feel happy for Hailey the second, even though I knew shortly after this last issue of *LL*, there would be a tragedy.

This one was the first and only time she appeared with anyone else in her pictures. All her other images were nude poses, or self-pleasure, but in *these* pictures, she was accompanied by a thick, chocolatey, hard-bodied partner whose face was always out of a frame.

His dick wasn't though.

That was prominent – in her hands, in her mouth, inside her. And it wasn't one sided — there were plenty of pictures where we couldn't see his face because it was buried between her legs, planted between her ass cheeks.

I *loved* it.

"Go ahead Hailey," I murmured, squinting as I leaned in a bit to see the caption. All of them carried the same one, simply *"The Exploration of the Bees"*.

"But what does that *mean* though?" I asked aloud, as if she could hear me.

I stared at the pictures a bit longer, discovering something new each time my eyes came back to a frame. I wasn't turned on, exactly, I was *fascinated*.

It was like looking at my past self, getting plowed.

Beautifully, though.

Beside me, the timer went off on my phone, indicating that my self-imposed period for research on *this* story was over.

It was time for me to get back to the thing with *Night Shift*. A few nights had passed now since Ellis introduced me to Laken and Keris at the bar, and they'd given me a great vibe.

They were excited about the prospect of the story, and had even invited me to join Ellis at their wedding. He told me later that had caught him off guard too – that they must have really gotten good energy from *me*, since they'd been stingy so far with the plus-ones.

I was honored, but this was another new thing for me.

Really *connecting* with people, and getting settled into where I was... this was *new*. Not that bonding with people, making base level friendships had ever been *hard* for me, but this was feeling different.

Deeper.

And not just new people either — I'd checked in with my long-distance friends a bit more than I normally would, and Cameron and I were becoming better home girls, even with me having known her for a long time. We went on a double date with the guys since they already knew each other, and worked together too.

I kind of had a blast.

Who knew?

It was over a laughter-filled lunch with her that I introduced the idea of giving the Kimbles and *Night Shift* the cover story whenever my piece about them ran. If they were into it, it would be lovely to get photos from the wedding, and they would probably lose their shit if I could secure Rashad Martin. His work was more editorial than lifestyle, but looking like they did, the Kimbles were editorial people.

"I *love* it," Cameron had assured me. "Consider Rashad ninety percent secured. I've got to see what him and Bianca are up to —he's been on sabbatical. Paternity leave."

I raised my eyebrows. "*Really?* I am obsessed with that," I laughed. "People change."

"Bianca made a man out of him," Cameron laughed. "Because if they'd had this name for it back then, honey, Rashad was a *fuckboy supreme*. He has grown all the way up."

I nodded, thinking about how fine his young ass had turned out over the last few years. "He sure as hell has. Milk did that body *good*," we laughed together, and then went on about finishing our lunches.

Instead of working from the *Sugar&Spice* offices for the rest of the day, I took my work back to the hotel with me after popping in to check on the house. There *was* progress, at least.

Angela had assured me her feelings about Ellis and I being involved would not affect her work, and Ellis had mirrored the same certainty.

I wasn't believing it until I saw it.

My knowledge of human nature dictated I maintain my cautiousness because love, feelings, and all of that... it was messy.

As hell.

I didn't want to be caught up with some nonsense, and luckily that didn't seem to be the case.

But I was watching.

I spent the rest of the afternoon working, and when I finally came up for air, it was nearly seven. Ellis was neck deep in another of those forever shifts, so it was time for another solo dinner, which I didn't mind.

Gave me an opportunity to think while I ate.

That "thinking" didn't last past the arrival of my entrée.

I felt a disturbance in the atmosphere.

Sure enough, when I looked up, my mother was strolling towards my table, looking pissed.

Great, as always, but pissed.

"Mama," I greeted her, standing to kiss her cheek. "To what do I owe your disdain today? And in *person* at that?" I asked.

"Really, Hailey?" she said, lowering herself into a seat across from me. "Can you let go of the snark for five minutes at least?"

"Now why would I do that, when you've taught me so well? I'm a testament to your mothering," I gushed.

She smirked. "Yes, you certainly are... Perrier please, and whatever passes for the salmon salad in this place," she said to the server who'd approached the table.

"It's a vegan restaurant mama", I told her, taking the burden of that explanation before the server had to. "She'll do the *Rabbit Food*," I said. "With citrus vinaigrette."

"Rabbit food?" my mother commented as soon as the server walked off. "What the hell is that?"

"It's a salad mama. Heirloom tomatoes, English cucumber, kalamata olives, red onion, croutons. A salad."

"So you're *vegan* now too?" She asked, and I laughed.

"The *restaurant* is vegan. I eat good food. Why do you say it like it's some scandal or something?"

"Not a scandal, just another similarity to your *dear father*, of course. Any distancing you can do from me, you take full advantage of."

"But I *just* told you it's not that. Why do you have to make everything about you?"

"You've done therapy, right?" she asked.

I lifted an eyebrow. "What does that have to do with anything?"

"Well, if you've been to therapy, you know, everything is always the mother's fault."

I nodded. "Of course. *You* are the actual victim here."

"As a matter of fact, I am, Hailey. But as many victims are wont to do, I've also played the role of villain. That's why I'm here," she explained.

"How did you find me anyway?" I asked, too curious to let it go. "It's not like I've been on social media, or anything like that. You got people watching me or something?"

"I've told you before, sweetheart, I've got eyes everywhere."

"Creepy."

"You call it creepy, I call it protective. Because believe it or not, I care about your well-being."

"I don't doubt that at all," I told her. "I also understand that there's a limit to it. I can be well, but only within *your* parameters. Anytime I step outside your narrow definitions of what *I'm* supposed to be, of what my *life* is supposed to mean, it's like I've made an enemy of you. I'm forty years old, Mama. I'm over feeling like that. I've *been* over feeling like that."

"Really?! By the way you speak to me, I never would have thought so," she replied dryly, as her salad was delivered to the table. I knew she wouldn't say anything else until she'd taken a few bites of her food, so I gave my attention to mine for a few minutes as well.

As much as I could.

There were many ways in which my mother was a predictable person. I'd known her all my life. But showing up in Blackwood, after being so adamantly against it?

This was something I hadn't expected.

And I didn't know what was happening next.

"I want to tell you a story," she said, after a few moments had passed without her rejecting the salad I suggested. "About a broken woman who showed up in a new city with nothing but the clothes on her back, and a small bag with a few belongings. She wasn't *broke* – in fact, by the standards of that time, she was quite wealthy. A rarity for a single, negro woman. Never married, no children, but running from something — from violence, heartache, fear. Putting as much distance between herself and her previous life as she could."

"Who is this story about, Mama?" I asked, even though I already had a pretty strong feeling.

"Hailey the second," she confirmed. "She went to California, and no one really knew who she was. Because the life she'd been living before, that was very much a local thing. Especially the magazine. Some people had probably sent a copy here and there to a relative somewhere else, but mostly, once it was gone, it was gone. Buried history. And she never *had* to talk about it, so she rarely did. She went back to business – dressing Black brides, and was very successful at that, as all her other endeavors have been. She met someone who wanted to marry her, but she refused. She wouldn't marry this man, but she had his children."

"One of which was Granny," I said, and my mother nodded.

"Yes, one of which was your grandmother. Now, your grandmother was heavily influenced by what she saw growing up at her mother's feet in that bridal shop. She saw beautiful Black women, from different walks of life, coming to *find their fit with Freeman's*. She wanted that for herself, desperately, because to her, it looked like the epitome of happiness. Her mother cried sometimes, and from a child's eyes, it looked like loneliness and regret. But those brides? Only ever tears of joy. She internalized it."

"And the societal pressure back *then* of marriage equaling victory..." I shook my head. "It was an obsession."

One she'd even tried to push on *me* before.

I shut her down though.

"Exactly," Mama agreed. "She grew up, got older, but that didn't really change her outlook – she wanted *nothing* more than to be married. And she found her husband, too, she thought. This boy she liked only wanted a good God-fearing woman, and she *had* to be from an upstanding family. Now, the money was there, but the "morals" not so much. Not with an unmarried woman who was "known" to get around at the head of the business and household. Your granny *begged* her mother to please find a husband, so that *she* could be seen as eligible. So, Hailey Freeman sat her daughter down for a talk. She explained that she *never* wanted to marry again, because her heart still belonged to the man who'd lost his life protecting her in the riots. He was the love of her life, and losing him... she never got past it. She was not interested in loving anybody else, wasn't interested in any parts of the life she'd had back in SugarLeaf. Including the hobbies and side business she'd glossed over in favor of talking about the tailoring business that the original Hailey Freeman had started. She shared these details hoping to connect with her daughter. But they had the opposite effect."

I shook my head, thinking about my holy roller grandmother, and how we'd had to revoke her social media access to keep her from burning the bridal business to the ground with offensive, antiquated views.

"Your grandmother was very upset, and went to her beau to tell him these things, thinking he would support her. He'd sworn to her they would get married, have a family, it was just a matter of getting past this hurdle of her family being good enough. But when he heard these fresh developments – heard about what Hailey the second had done... he dropped her. Told her he couldn't marry into a family like that. The only problem was, she was already pregnant."

"With...*you*, I guess," and she nodded.

"Yes, with me."

"Wow," I huffed. "Your daddy was trash. Cause how the hell is he worried about morals and marrying into good "Christian" families while he's getting a woman he's not married to pregnant?"

My mother shrugged. "That's the kind of thing people do all the time. Selective "holiness". And unfortunately, what your grandmother took away from that experience was that this was not information for *anyone* to know...this was information to be ashamed of. She raised me with no help from my father – she grudgingly accepted her mother's resources though. Years later, she found love with my brother's father, but that didn't work out either. I was never clear about what happened, but I know she blamed this on *being* an unwed mother, and *coming from* an unwed mother. She had this idea that there was this... repugnance in our family's past, that needed to be buried. She decided she was going to change our whole trajectory."

"I feel like she needed therapy."

"That's likely," Mama agreed. "But... time went on." She said with a sad smile. "Believe it or not Hailey, we are *very* much alike. Or at least, we used to be. All that holy stuff your grandmother was talking about, I went along with it, but really I didn't want to hear much about that. *Especially* once I met *your* father. Sexiest man I'd ever laid my eyes on — never met *anyone* that made me feel the way he did, just walking into a room. I was obsessed... and so was he," she said, smiling about it. "Did he ever tell you he asked to marry me?"

My eyes went wide. "*No*," I breathed. "Never."

She nodded. "No, I'm sure he wouldn't have. I broke his heart. Because my mother, through rage and tears, on the verge of a total meltdown, absolutely *begged* me. An *artist*, Chelle? *Really. A hippie? How is this man going to build a life for you and your future children? Do you really think he's going to be stable? Don't you know what happens to people like him? The alcohol? The drugs?*" she stopped, shaking her head. "You have to understand—my mother was my *everything*. She was all I ever consistently had. Mama Hailey had died when I was a young girl, and so again... she was all I knew. I felt like I owed it to my mother to make a stable decision about my life. So I gave your father back his ring," she revealed, clearing her throat to check the sudden emotion in her voice. "And I started dating someone she approved of. A young man whose family owned a resort out in Owens Harbor. He was a decent guy — he was handsome enough, smart enough, nice enough, except... shortly after we started dating, I found out I was pregnant. With you."

"Oh, *shit*."

"So of course I couldn't continue with this relationship. And my mother..." she shook her head. "Upset doesn't even describe it. Your father, when I told him... he begged me to come back to him, wanted to be together, but I still felt so beholden to Mama, who'd sacrificed her reputation to have me. Supposedly. I think she thought my father would come back to her once I was born, but... that's a whole other story. As for me —she wanted me to have the abortion *she* didn't have. That was the one thing I refused to do though. Not when... I was in love with your father. I didn't want to destroy my only proof of what we'd felt. I could still have you, and *then* I could find someone, could start dating again, and be with someone who was mama approved. That never happened. They were *never* Mama approved. And eventually they could never earn *my* approval for very long, either. It's a trait I'm afraid I've passed down to you."

I sucked my teeth. "No, these men are asinine," I told her, reaching across the table to clasp her hand. "There's nothing wrong with *us* for not wanting them. They're awful, and we don't have to look past it anymore cause we can own land and have bank accounts."

"Hailey!"

"What?" I shrugged. "It's true. Not that women are perfect, but we're a lot better than *them*."

"I'm glad you can joke about it Hailey, but I'm being serious."

"So am I."

"*Hailey.*"

"Sorry."

She gave me one more *look*, and I pretended to zip my lips so she could speak.

"After our phone conversation the other day, I kept thinking about what you said about feeling so alone, and disconnected. I've... felt that too. We've used what we deemed the good parts of your great-grandmother and her foremother's lives as motivation, and elevation, as a feel-good story to build this business on. While depriving you of the genuine history of your family, and leaving you disconnected from a legacy that's in your blood. And I'm sorry," she said, shocking the hell out of me. "I'm sorry for not being strong

enough to defy my mother's wishes for you. My last real act of
rebellion was naming you Hailey. She was furious, but it was too late
to change it at that point. I thought we could change the discourse. I
thought it was this thing, that eventually she would come to see as a
positive that she would look at you, this sweet baby girl, with the
same name as the mother she unfairly despised and be able to see it
differently. I thought it would soften her."

"I don't think that worked…"

"Oh, it definitely didn't," Mama agreed. "It made her harder on
me, which made me harder on you. Something you said, about our
mistake being that we thought honor needed to be restored to the
Freeman name in the first place… that broke my heart. Because it
wasn't as if it was this new concept, but I thought about how trying to
hide from that history, and being ashamed of it, has turned our family
legacy into something else. Yes, on the outside, we have a successful
bridal business founded by a woman who escaped the atrocities of
slavery to find success and freedom. But on the inside… I don't think
I've ever been as free as even the *first* Hailey Freeman was, not
mentally. Or the second Hailey Freeman, posing for those pictures,
writing those stories. Or…even you, my dear. You never let anybody
shutter your spirit. And as much as this has *frustrated* me," she
sighed. "Deep down… it has also always been a source of intense
pride. You've never had a problem standing up for yourself, even to
me. And I'm grateful that somehow, you could find the strength I
could never grasp for myself," She sat back, and shrugged. "Who
knows — maybe I should've been thanking your *damn daddy* after
all."

I shook my head. "Nope. Not him – that stubbornness and
strength is all *you*. I can't pretend to know what would have been
happening in your head, or the intricacies of your relationship with
Granny. But I've always seen you as strong. Running the business,
taking charge, reviving it to bring it back from mismanagement.
Never letting a man take advantage of you, *or* me. Remember that
one guy — you *begged* me not to tell Daddy after I told you he was

looking at me, saying stuff to me. I was what, fifteen, something like that? I was so hurt, thinking you were just trying to quiet me, that you didn't believe me, or worse—you didn't care. You invited him to our house, and you told me I *had* to come out and sit with y'all. And you beat his ass with that umbrella. I've never forgotten that."

"My shoulder ain't been the same *since*," Mama laughed. "I bet he thought twice before he tried to mess with another little girl though."

"I sure hope so," I shook my head. "And for the record, I realized as an adult that you made me promise not to tell Daddy because you didn't want him to kill him."

"You needed your daddy present in your life, not in jail. Of course... it would have made him less of a pain in *my* ass."

"I never understood why you and Daddy didn't get along," I laughed. "I mean like... later on. He never said a cross word about you. I'm pretty sure he loved you, still."

Mama sighed. "And that's exactly why," she revealed. "He did. And I... I didn't know how to accept that. after everything, after so long. It was easier to be mad and keep him at a distance."

"That is probably one of the most frustrating things I've ever heard," I told her.

"Try experiencing it," she laughed, and then reached into her purse.

I frowned at the worn pouch she slid across the table to me.

"What is this?"

"Open it."

I reach for the pouch, opening it up to reveal a leather-bound journal inside, with a name embossed on the front.

Hailey Freeman.

"Your grandmother doesn't know I have this," she explained. "It was among a bunch of stuff she destroyed, years and years ago. Before you were even born. Thinking back, I wish I had done more, wish I tried to stop her from destroying all of Hailey's things. But this was after her relationship with your uncles's father had fallen apart, and I think she was especially angry with her mother. Needed someone, *anyone,* to blame. She made a big bonfire out in the yard, burned it all. But I took that away, tucked it under my dress and I kept it. I hid it in my bedroom, and I don't know what for, cause I was certainly too young to really know what I was doing. Probably eleven or twelve years old. I opened it, looked at it, but I never read it. I'm not even sure its readable anymore. But I still had it. And... I thought you might want it."

When I flipped it open, I quickly realized I was looking at one of Hailey the second's journals. There were a couple in the box of things I'd gotten from the museum, but this one seemed significantly newer than those, which had been written when she was a much younger woman. A quick glance at the first few pages confirmed that this was Hailey in California.

After the riots, after the move.

"Thank you," I whispered, in awe of not only the fact that this had been kept, and so well preserved, but that my mother had been willing to give it to me.

"You're welcome," she told me. "Now. When can we go see this house?"

Momentarily, since we were in what felt like a good place, I considered telling her about Ellis, and Angela, and ... *everything*.

Self-preservation won though.

I got the scoop on how long she was staying, her flight details and all that, and then assured I would make time the next day to show her the house. We could go over the plans, and hell... I might even let her make a few changes.

If she was interested, I would not deny her this access, because this was *her* history, too. If it wasn't for the influence of my grandmother, this journey with the house could have been *hers*.

Hopefully, with less fire.

Back up in my room, after we'd parted ways, I tried to tell myself to wait until the next day to crack open the journal since I was exhausted.

That didn't happen.

With my book light turned up bright, wearing a pair of archival gloves I'd gotten from Collette when I picked up the other things, I went back to that first page of the journal and started poring over the words.

It was from when she first settled in California— her musings on the differences in the people, the culture, the fashion, race relations, all of that. But there was this certain melancholy to her I easily attributed to sorrow over having to move, having to rebuild.

But then, something there reminded me of what my mother had said – Hailey the second left Sugarleaf with her heart broken. I skipped to some later parts of the journal, and that was where I found it – one particular passage confirming it.

She was still in mourning for a man who was killed in the massacre.

She wasn't even able to bury him, no memorial, no *closure*. He was shot right in front of her, and the only reason she didn't stay with him until he died was because he begged her not to.

He begged her to go home, to grab a bag, to *run*.

So she did.

I do not know if it was a blessing or a curse that I did not wait there with my love until he had grown cold. It was chaotic that day, terrifying and consuming, and I always trusted my love to never steer me wrong. Leaving him there with our bloods mixing from our wounds, his grave, mine shallow, was my last act of obedience to the man I never had the honor of calling my husband. These Californians do not understand why they cannot turn my head, and the women think I am putting on airs. But it is not that I think too much of myself – I am not myself. I am not whole. And I cannot simply tell them, because to do so would be to reduce what should have been the love of a lifetime to an unremarkable footnote.

I was not supposed to be alone, and what makes it worse is that I do not even get the esteem and respect, the room to grieve that would normally be offered to a widow.

I feel like I am dying inside, and cannot move on from this place.
But I promised him I would go on.
I promised him I would keep living.
So I will.
However, the fact remains, I was supposed to be Mrs. Ellis Boyd.
And now that is a destiny that will never come to be.

I snapped the journal closed, eyes wide, mind spinning.

Then I flipped it open to read it again, because there was *no way* I read what I thought I had.

Could I have read what I thought I read?

No.

Right?

I quickly found the page again, skimming for that section.

And there it was, clearly penned in Hailey the second's beautiful script.

Absolutely haunting words that made no sense.

I was supposed to be Mrs. Ellis Boyd.

FOURTEEN

ELLIS

"HEY BOYD, YOU GOOD?"

The truthful answer was *hell no*, but I threw on a neutral expression before turning to my captain to nod.

"Yeah," I lied, but Will crossed his arms, leaning into the doorway of the bunk room to make sure I knew he didn't believe it. Everybody else was... somewhere else. Like this collective agreement to give me a little space I hadn't actually asked for.

After a moment, he shook his head. "Jai sent over dinner," he said, referring to his sister-in-law—owner and head chef over at Honeybee. It was one of our favorite restaurants, the kind of place you needed a reservation to get in at dinner time. So her sending those meals for the entire squad wasn't something to take lightly.

It was always after something big had zapped us.

Like a massive drunk driving accident that took way too many lives.

Like today.

"You ever wonder what it would be like if we actually *could* save them all when shit like this happened?" I asked. "Like we show up, everything is fucked, but then..."

"We save the day for everybody?" Will filled in for me, chuckling. "It's a great fantasy, but we know it's not usually our reality."

"Yeah, I just... *shit*. That man that lost both of his kids..."

Will nodded, stepping into the room. "I know. It's rough when we see people lose their families. But what you're feeling right now... is it because *he* lost them? Or because *you* did?"

I dropped my gaze, propping my chin on my hands as the scene played out in my mind.

If I'd noticed him sooner.

If I'd moved faster.

The situation on the highway was a disaster.

A large part of our task when we first arrived was working with the police and the other engine that had responded to get uninjured people and onlookers out of the way so that people who needed medical attention could get it. A lot of the injuries were minor, some not so much. We divided and conquered – teams of two, at least one with EMS certifications. Working that way, we could hasten through the scene, vehicle by vehicle to check on the occupants.

It was getting dark fast, which only complicated our efforts at rescue and recovery – visibility was a bitch. It was out of the corner of my eye that I saw this man waving to get our attention as he climbed up the embankment, seemingly unable to speak. Flailing, panicked, trying desperately to catch somebody's interest.

How long has he been trying to get help?

When I noticed him, I went to him, listening intently as he gasped out that his kids were stuck in the car. A quick glance at the destroyed railing nearby led me in the right direction, and I rushed over to see where he was pointing.

An overturned vehicle, smoking in the concrete drain.

Smashed up so badly I wasn't even sure how *he'd* gotten out.

I tasked my paramedic teammate with seeing about the father – my first move was back to the truck, to grab the heavy-duty equipment I'd need to get me through that metal trap to get his children out. On the way, I flagged down another team, yelling over the noise to let them know what we needed to do.

We didn't make it back down the embankment before the vehicle caught on fire.

It wasn't like in the movies where the car explodes in a ball of fire so intense it blows you back and leaves you reeling.

No, our feet were firmly planted in our heavy boots as the sudden, overwhelming rush of heat hit us at the same time as the wave of horror – we were too far away to do much of anything about it as flames engulfed the car.

That didn't stop us from trying, but we all knew it was too late.

"I don't know if I can stomach dinner right now," I told Will, not answering his question. "Next shift is here in like thirty minutes—"

"Go ahead," Will said, not even waiting for me to finish the question I was about to ask, because he already knew.

I needed to get the hell out of there.

I took myself straight to the location that had quickly become synonymous with solace for me – Hailey's hotel. I chuckled a bit as I approached her room door, thinking about the first day she'd giving me this key card, and the workout it'd gotten since then.

It was early as hell in the morning, and as expected, she was asleep. I went through my usual routine of a long shower and a bit of meditation before I joined her in the bed.

Usually, she snuggled right up to me. I'd even teased her about it, since she was the one who was holding back more between the two of us.

Today she didn't immediately respond.

I knew she was awake because of the shift in her breathing, so I flipped her over onto her back and planted myself over her.

"I pissed you off again?" I asked. "What I do this time?"

"You haven't done anything," she replied with a heavy sigh. "What makes you think you pissed me off? Because I didn't immediately spread my legs for you?"

I raised an eyebrow at her, trying to meet her gaze in the faint early morning sunrays the curtains were filtering into the room. "Your whole energy is off, and you're gonna lie in my face like you're not being weird? That's where we are?" I asked. "Cause I can—"

"No," she said, finally looking at me. She reached up, fingers sliding along my facial hair for something much closer to the type of greeting I expected. "Do it now," she said, hiking her legs around my waist.

Something... was off.

But she was already wet, already ready for me, so I obliged her request, groaning at the sweetness of her pussy as it gripped around me. She pulled my face down to hers, and I indulged that too, dipping my tongue into the sweetness of her mouth for a deep kiss as I buried my dick as far into her as I could get. Her fingers went from my face to my back, digging in as I stroked.

"*Shit*," I muttered in her ear. "You're gonna fuck around and I'm gonna make you *Mrs. Boyd*," I teased, thinking it would make her laugh. I pulled back a bit, wanting to see her – wanting to watch the bounce of her breasts, the pleasure play out on her face... but she wouldn't meet my gaze anymore.

Physically, that wasn't something that presented a problem — the mechanics of what we were doing simply were what they were. I got her there, and then got myself there, but it wasn't as intimate as what I'd become used to. It was functional, which was fine, but it was ... Weird.

And not at all what I had arrived needing from her.

"You sure we're good?" I asked, after we were done and had cleaned up. "If I upset you somehow, you know you can tell me that, right?" I probed, cupping her chin to encourage her to meet my eyes.

She blew out a sigh. "You haven't done anything. I'm sorry. I've got a lot on my mind. Are *you* good?" she asked, genuinely. "You seem a little down."

I shrugged. "Nothing I shouldn't be used to by now."

"We get *used to* fucked up things all the time," she countered. "What's going on?"

"Just a bad shift," I answered, knowing that keeping it to myself was pretty useless.

"That accident, on the freeway?"

I nodded.

"Oh *no*," she said, immediately wrapping her arms around me – one around my shoulders, the other hand cradling my head as she pulled me into her chest.

Damn.

Now *this* was what I needed.

She didn't even say anything else, didn't ask for any details I wasn't interested in giving. She just held me like that, quietly, her fingernails tracing a steady back and forth behind my ear. Like I was a damn baby.

I couldn't front.

I loved every second of that shit.

We stayed like that until she had to get to work, and I traded her comforting for my mother's, who started feeding me as soon as I walked through her front door.

"How did you know?" I asked her, and she waved me off.

"You know your daddy still be listening on the scanner," she reminded me. "And anyway, a mama *knows*. Including about this young lady you been sneaking around town with, like you can't tell anybody."

"I haven't been *sneaking* around town with her, Mama," I said, over a mouthful of sweet potatoes. "I'm not quite ready to make that introduction yet. Wait — that's a lie. I don't think *she's* ready for that introduction yet. So we're going to give it a little more time."

"Okay, but make sure she knows—she got to get *my* stamp of approval first."

I gave my mama a playful eye roll, because, "Come on woman, you know you like everybody."

"I don't like *everybody*," she argued, and I hit her with twisted lips, because *maybe* it wasn't *everybody*, but she could certainly find something good to say about ninety-nine percent of the population.

Well, ninety-nine percent of Black folks.

"You taking her to the beer wedding?" my father asked, and I nodded, chuckling over his categorization.

"Yep, she is going to be my date."

"You think she gonna be in there knocking them other girls out the way to catch the bouquet?" my father joked, and I couldn't do anything except laugh right with him.

"Never mind *that* – have you prepared her for going to a wedding with you?" My mama asked, sliding a big ass serving of peach cobbler in front of me, no matter that it was nine in the morning and I'd already eaten a full Sunday dinner-esque plate.

I frowned. "What do you mean, have I *prepared* her for it?"

She exchanged a look with my father, and he was the one to answer. "Boy you know your ass gets emotional at weddings," my father ribbed. "Ever since you were a little boy. What's the cry count up to now?"

"*Daaaamn*, this how y'all do your only child?"

They *laughed*.

"Answer the question, boy," my mama insisted.

I put my fork down. "I do not *cry* at weddings," I argued. "I shed a few heartfelt, silent, *very masculine* tears. Three max. Six if its great vows. Eight to ten if they get somebody up there singing. Not like that banshee Collette had."

"*That was her sister-in-law,*" my mother whisper-yelled, as if we were gossiping in public or something.

I had a good time laughing back and forth with them about my supposed weakness for weddings before my father dropped a bit of knowledge on me.

"You know you get that from your great-granddaddy, right?" he asked. "He never got married, but oh *man*, was he a sucker for love. I loved my granddaddy – good man," he declared. "He's the reason I became a firefighter, *and* that I could marry your mama. You know my daddy had passed before I even met her, and I was a little rascal. She made me want to get in line, and your great-granddaddy taught me what I needed to do to keep a woman like this on my side. He lost the love of his life, and he never recovered from it. He didn't want that to happen to me."

I nodded, but... "If he was such a big believer in love, why did he never get married himself? How did he lose the *love of his life*?"

My father sighed. "He didn't really like talking about it, but I know it has something to do with those riots up here back in the day."

My eyebrows went up, thinking about how that same historical event had been on my mind so much lately because of Hailey's deep familial connection.

"Those devils shot your great-granddaddy and left him in the street for dead. But I'm here now, and *you* here now – named you after him."

I chuckled. "Yeah, you've made sure I knew about that great honor – but I don't think you've ever mentioned him getting shot in the riots? Surviving a gunshot wound back then? How was that even possible?" I said, turning to my mother, the former nurse, thinking she might have some insight.

She shrugged. "Bullet hit the right spot, I guess," she answered, shaking her head. "Definitely a marvel. He was a lucky man."

"He sure was," my father said, nodding. "I mean, look at my own damn brother! Look at Franklin!"

My mother pushed out a sigh and mumbled something along the lines of *here we go* under her breath as she got up and started clearing the table.

"What you mean here we go?" my father countered, as if we weren't all perfectly clear on what she meant.

Here he fuckin' went.

There was no love lost between Franklin and my father, even though the men were brothers. Franklin was a veteran who had been injured in combat, and came back home a shell of himself in countless ways – mentally, physically, emotionally.

At first, my father had been nothing but supportive of his brother, trying his best to be a resource to him and his family, like he and my mother were for so many others. It went well – Reva and I became close because she was at my house all the time, the two of us looking out for each other because of our parent's schedules. Her mother worked with mine at the hospital, and my father was right at Franklin's side while he was trying to find work and get further education. Eventually, he ended up training as a firefighter, which he became.

I still wasn't sure that was the best course of action for him though.

His combat PTSD was only exacerbated by the stress and trauma of fighting fires, and back in those days, especially for a Black man, protecting your mental health was basically unheard of.

You were supposed to "tough it out".

He turned to self-medicating to get himself through it, and what started as a little joint here and there to take the edge off, cocktailed with alcohol abuse, eventually stopped working for him. His substance abuse became worse and worse as he needed more and more to take the pain away.

That was when his life *really* started falling apart. It definitely wasn't due to lack of familial support. My parents had tried, Reva's mother had tried, Reva had tried, *I* tried. Now that we were all adults, I was the only one who even still tried to engage him.

But ultimately, lasting change was going to be up to Franklin himself.

That was something that had been drilled into me by Laken, whose brother had gone through something similar. Eventually, an overdose had claimed his brother's life, but Laken was never foul about it.

He *always* spoke about his brother with grace and compassion, which helped me navigate some of my relationship with Franklin. It taught me to avoid treating the man like he was some lost cause, not human anymore.

But I knew that my father and Reva had a completely different

AFFAIR 145

relationship with him than I did, and they'd been hurt by him on a different level.

Especially Reva.

So I tried my best to walk that tightrope whenever I needed to.

Today, I didn't see a need. I changed the damn subject, because I wasn't trying to get my father riled up. I wanted to keep the tone light, because that was the headspace where I wanted to be.

I maintained that energy too, all the way up to Laken's wedding. There was a public opening of the barrel, tasting of the beer — which was impeccable by the way, even straight out the barrel, so I knew it was going to be even better once we got it kegged and chilled on tap.

After that though, learning that our experiment with the Kimble bourbon barrels had been a success, it was time for the real celebration – the nuptials that were happening once everyone had been funneled out in the bar, and we'd closed it except for the friends and family who were gathered to witness.

"A *second* marriage," I ribbed Laken, tapping my glass of *Henry's Renaissance* to his. "How you feel?"

"I feel good as hell, man," he grinned. "The vast majority of people don't get a second chance, and I'm planning to make the absolute most of mine with my *fine ass* wife."

"I heard that man," I agreed, looking over to where a happy Keris was surrounded by women, one of them being Hailey, who she seemed to have hit it off with.

"I see how you've been looking at your lady all night El," Laken spoke up. "I might be on my second, but uh... what about you and your first? You thinking Hailey might be that one?"

I chuckled, shaking my head. "Man... as insane as it is, I think... shit, maybe so? I've actually thought so since the beginning," I admitted. "But again, I know that's crazy."

Laken shrugged. "You know me–if it's right, it's right. We can say all this stuff about how long you're supposed to know someone, what it's supposed to look like, all of that. But I really believe...when you know, *you know*. And for most people, that takes time. So if you telling me you *knew* off bat? Sounds like a sign to me, my man."

I nodded. "Yeah, maybe so."

Laken excused himself to go talk to his new wife, and I took the opportunity to pull Hailey aside, making sure she was good too. Yes, she was a grown woman, but this was still a room full of people I knew, but *she* mostly didn't.

She sure as hell *looked* good, and I was still miffed she hadn't let me take advantage of it earlier, insisting she didn't want me having her looking *"well fucked"* at the wedding. She tried to act like she didn't like my *what better place to look like that* comment, but she laughed, so she wasn't fooling nobody.

"How is it going? You doing okay?" I asked her, and she grinned.

"Well, the photographer has gotten some amazing shots, including one I'm sure is going to be the cover, so *thrilled* there. And I talked to Marlene, Laken's mother." She stopped to give a fake pout. "We are *not* descended from the same Freemans, which was a teensy bit disappointing, but she still made my entire night. Check this out — Marlene got married in a Freeman bridal dress!"

My eyes went wide. "You're kidding me!"

"Nope! She went all the way to California, and *found her fit with Freeman*," she laughed. "With *Hailey* Freeman! She actually remembers her – told me I look like her! And you want to know something else?" she gushed. "You see that beautiful white lace bespoke tie Laken is wearing? And the matching hair piece, and Keris' top? They're *all* custom pieces, using Marlene's Freeman bridal veil," Hailey told me, grinning. "All these little details, this history weaved in – hello, the beer named after Laken's father, aged in family bourbon barrels?! It is … *amazing*. This was beautiful. Thank you for having me on your arm tonight."

I scoffed. "Nah, thank you for *being* on my arm tonight. If it wasn't for you, I wouldn't have a date. I'd be out here looking lonely."

Hailey smirked. "Somehow I doubt that. I am *quite* sure you could have found some woman who would have been downright thrilled to accompany you to these festivities tonight."

"True," I admitted, "but *you* are the only woman I would have been comfortable seeing my thug tears about my homeboy marrying the love of his life tonight."

She laughed. "You know, I *wanted* to want to talk about you, but... it was a beautiful ceremony. You can tell those two are really all about each other. It's wonderful."

"*Exactly*," I agreed. "The vows, the first dance, the cake, all that. I love weddings, I can't help it. It's funny — my pops was *just* telling me how he thinks it's some kind of like, inherited trait from my great grandfather." I snapped my fingers. "*Oh!* I was going to mention— you're not the only one named after your great-grandparent," I told Hailey, whose eyes went wide.

"Huh?"

"You remember, you were telling me about how you were named after Hailey Freeman, who was named after Hailey Freeman?"

She nodded. "Yeah, of course."

"Well, *I* was named after my great-grandfather, Ellis. Making me the second Ellis." I scoffed. "You've still got me beat though, since you're the *third* Hailey."

Hailey raised her hands, shaking her head. "Wait a minute — Ellis Boyd was your *great-grandfather*? Not like... a great uncle, or something?"

"Nah," I answered, confused. "Definitely my great-grandfather."

"How?"

I frowned. "What do you mean, how? Do you... know him or something?" I asked, and then my eyes went wide. "Oh, *shit!* Did he know your great-grandmother? Ah, *hell,* my great-granddaddy got his dick out in the magazine, don't he?"

Hailey shook her head, brushing off my barrage of words. "Wait, Ellis. Please back up! I thought Ellis Boyd died in the riots in Sugarleaf. He was *shot.* Like, a mortal wound."

I nodded. "Yeah, he was," I said. "But he didn't die. It was a grave injury, but...," I shrugged, lifting my arms to tell her like my father had said a couple days ago, "Here I am, *definitely* descended from him. He was my father's grandfather. Raised him and his brother after his father passed away. Are you going to answer my question about the magazine though?"

Absently, Hailey shook her head, backing away. "I... I've got to go," she blurted, and turned to presumably rush out, but I caught her hand, pulling her back towards me.

"Hold up now," I said. "Don't run off on me, Hailey. Tell me what the hell is going on."

She shook her head. "I can't *tell* you. I... I have to show you."

FIFTEEN

HAILEY

GIVING IN TO ALL THIS WAS NEVER SUPPOSED TO BE AN OPTION.

As long as I held *something* back, it made it all so much easier to pretend that I *wasn't* inextricably wrapped up in Ellis.

At this point though, who was I fooling?

Even before seeing his name printed in Hailey the second's journal, I knew I was looking forward to seeing him too much, relied too heavily on his quiet company while I was working, enjoyed too many meals, indulged in too much intoxicating sex.

And sticking around after that Angela thing?

Unheard of.

Not that it was *that* big of a deal, but if it was big enough to piss me off, it was big enough to kill the situation – at least that had always been the case before.

Now, I was.... *Lost.*

With no desire of working my way out of whatever maze this was, and my God – what a scary feeling.

Would I even feel like this if it wasn't for the journal?

Yes.

When I asked myself that question in the car, after we'd left the wedding and were silently heading back to *Eden*, I could easily answer, with full certainty.

Because the journal wasn't a catalyst – it was confirmation.

Spirituality and all that was way over my head, but even I had to admit – there had always been something peculiar about my connection with Ellis. To come into contact with a stranger you've never laid eyes on, and instantly feel like you'd known them for *so* long?

There was something to it.

I definitely believed in instant connections – there was nothing strange about quickly, easily hitting it off with someone. But now, with the borderline supernatural details of all this – my great-grandmother knowing – and *loving* – his great-grandfather, only to be torn apart, and then, a hundred years later...

What if that's what *all* "fast friends" and "love at first sight" situations were?

Just a reconnection of past kindred spirits?

Really, Hailey?

I shook my head, trying to brush it all off, but that was impossible. Not with all these facts laid out in front of me, and Ellis clueless to all of it.

I hadn't mentioned anything to Collette yet, since his revelation that they were loosely related. I didn't need anything traveling up the grapevine before he and I had figured this all out.

Not that I knew what there might be to "figure out".

I didn't *do* being in love.

Hell, I didn't do *relationships*.

I barely did *situationships*, because I was so easily over it and ready to move on.

But what if – like Ellis – it was always because it wasn't the right person, and I *knew* that, so there was never a need to waste time? Just get the physical desires filled, and keep trucking on.

What if it was always because nobody else was... *him*.

The implications of that were... *so much*.

Too much.

So *too much* that even though the reasoning for coming to the hotel was me supposedly telling him – showing him – everything once we got to my room, that was the last thing I wanted to do.

Especially when I didn't know how he'd react to any of it.

Did I believe he was into me?

Yes, without question.

But to go from that to, *hey, I think the reason we've felt so familiar to each other was because our ancestors didn't get to fully realize their love in the way they wanted, and we're their reincarnated souls who found each other a hundred years later,* was maybe... a lot.

Not maybe.

It definitely was.

"Do you still want me like you did earlier?" I asked him, as soon as we were on the other side of the door, in my room.

Already half out of his suit jacket, Ellis looked at me like I was crazy before replying, "Uh... hell yeah. But I thought you wanted to tal—"

Nope.

I quieted that with a kiss, pushing my body against his body, my tongue into his mouth, before he could even finish the sentence.

It wasn't about distracting him, not really.

His distraction was merely a perk of my *own.*

Still fully embroiled in a kiss, I sidled my hands between us, undoing his pants, pushing down his boxers, going for the shallow reminder of the physical connection between us.

Sex was so much easier to understand.

The dick on this man was magnificent – long, thick, beautifully veined.

Of course I felt a bond bordering on divine as I sank to my knees to take it down my throat, to adulate and admire while I gagged on it.

What dick-lover *wouldn't*?

I happily focused on making him curse and grunt and moan, his fingers digging into my hair to twist and tug as I sucked him off. With one hand, I fisted his dick, using my saliva as lubrication to stroke him hard. His balls were in my mouth, my other hand between my own legs as I cast my gaze upward to meet his. His eyes were half-closed, lips slightly parted.

Until I took his dick in my mouth again.

All the way down my throat, balls on my chin, deep as I could get, sucking him like I'd never get another chance to do so... like I was making up for lost time.

Like I'd missed him.

Then his eyes were shut tight, fingers in a vice grip on my hair, mouth wide open with fresh curses – all followed up with soft swipes of his thumbs under my eyes to wipe my cheeks, and a gentle caress under my chin. His gaze locked on mine, lips moving to tell me, while I was a mess of saliva and streaked mascara, *"You look so fucking beautiful like this."*

I thanked him for the compliment by sucking harder, in tandem with a finger across that stretch of skin behind his balls that made his hips buck, pushing him further down my throat.

That was all it took.

Moments later, his hands were back in my hair, holding me still while he fucked my face until he came with a ragged grunt and a warning I ignored in favor of swallowing every drop he spilled into my mouth.

I didn't have time to catch my breath before he'd joined me on the ground, pushing my thighs apart to get his face between them. I'd discovered quite early on that he held a very particular predilection for eating my pussy, in the messiest possible of ways. There was never a time his face wasn't soaked with me afterward – and never a time I didn't adore *every second*.

This was no different.

Actually... that wasn't true.

Just like I'd given my all in devotion on my knees, he did the same, an extra *oomph* to his tongue, his lips, his fingers. Maybe it was my imagination playing tricks on me, or maybe... maybe all the new information had me feeling more connected. Whatever the case was... the release was magnificent.

My eyes were half-closed, body spent from orgasm when Ellis climbed on top of me, lining his dick up to sink into me before he even bothered wiping his face. He still smelled like me when he lowered his face to mine, grazing my lips for a soft kiss.

"I love you," he murmured to me, and....

Shit.

Just like when he'd joked about marrying me... I didn't know what to do with how those words made me feel – didn't know what to do with the warmth in my chest, the unshed tears in my eyes, or... the desire to say it back.

The *need* to say it back.

Did I even feel it?

Or was this someone else's words, emotions, trying to break through?

... did it matter?

Maybe not.

Ellis had already moved on, trailing kisses up my neck as he rocked his hips into mine. We peeled out of the clothes as we went. His hands went behind my knees, pushing my legs up to hook over his shoulders. His fingers laced through my fingers, clasped and entwined as he stroked me, beautifully slow and deliciously deep, hitting all the exact right places.

Because he *knew* all the exact right places.

Because he knew *me*.

I *wanted* to focus on the moment, but my mind took me elsewhere, to all the time we'd spent together over the last few months. That whole *figuring each other out* phase was one we'd never had, because we already felt so familiar. It was easy to fall right into the comfortable patterns.

Easy to accept the other as they were.

There was no friction about work because we knew what the other required. We missed each other and were glad to get whatever time we had. When we *were* apart, he was on my mind – not to the point of distraction, but present. And his random texts throughout the day let me know it was mutual.

When we were together?

It was disgusting to me, truly, how much I relished it.

I couldn't remember *any* time another person made me feel like that. He always had stories, and was always interested in *my* stories, and always had a new place for us to try out. His energy gave *me* energy, and even as someone who'd traveled the world meeting people and experiencing things... it was crazy how he didn't even have to take me out of this city – or out, at all – to make me feel like I was doing something new.

It... sounded like the way my father talked about my mother.

It sounded like when Laken talked about Keris, when Cameron talked about Will.

It sounded like...

"I love you too," I blurted – *tried* to blurt.

It felt like Ellis was in my damn lungs so it was more like I panted it out between strokes, prompting him to stop, face twisted in momentary confusion before his lips spread into a smile.

A smile that lit up my whole damn world.

Yeah.

I was *definitely* gone in the head.

But... I felt like I could say with confidence that I wasn't alone – my words seemed to prompt Ellis to put a little extra into his stroke, to where I was a soaked, hollering mess by the time he finally pushed me off the cliff to another climax he almost immediately joined, with one last stroke that made my mind ... *staticky.*

It was amazing.

"Why do I feel like we should've... shit, recorded that," he chuckled in my ear. "For posterity or something. I feel like we looked good."

Okay.

Shit.

Afterglow over.

"I need to show you something," I said, pulling myself to sit up. His eyes immediately zeroed in on my breasts.

"I know, I neglected my friends. I've got y'all next time though," he declared, somehow keeping his expression neutral.

"I need to be serious right now," I told him, meeting his gaze so he'd know I really meant it.

He nodded. "Okay. But… you wanna shower first, or…?"

"Yeah," I agreed, grateful for another momentary reprieve. "Let's do that."

It didn't take nearly long enough.

What actually ended up happening was Ellis showering and brushing his teeth and dressing for bed in all his own stuff – another clue to how comfortable this thing between us had gotten, *very* quickly.

Before I could lose my nerve, I grabbed the most relevant copy of the magazine – one I'd purposely not shown him – handing him a pair of archival gloves to put on before putting the timeworn paper in his hands.

His eyes went wide. "Daaaamn – if I didn't know better, I'd definitely think this was you," he chuckled, looking at the pictures. "These pictures are a hundred years old, huh? And… damn, lucky man."

I didn't say anything.

I waited to see if anything would spark for him, without the other Ellis' face in the picture. At first, he seemed very amused by it, but his expression slowly shifted as he looked through all the pictures, then glanced up to ask me, "Hey… this guy… do you know who he is?"

"I do," I admitted, then pointed to the caption. "*The Exploration of the Bees*. I believe it's not about… *bees*, but more about the letter *B*. As in… the *Boyds*."

Ellis frowned. "What?"

I cleared my throat. "Based on what I've been able to research and all that, I think these pictures are a *very* intimate engagement shoot."

"So... you're telling me your great-grandmother married a Boyd? As in... *my* Boyds?"

"I'm telling you that my great-grandmother was engaged to... *Ellis Boyd*. They never got married though."

Ellis looked away from me, back to the magazine I'd put in his hands. "So... this is..."

"Hailey and Ellis. A hundred years ago."

His head kept moving in a subtle shake as he flipped through the images again. And then...

"That's..."

Insane?

Creepy?

"... kinda..."

Terrifying?

Impossible?

"Incredible," he murmured, with a soft chuckle that sent a tremendous wave of relief through me before he looked up, meeting my eyes again. "So... we *had* met before."

I mirrored his quiet laugh and nodded. "Yeah... I guess so."

"And you're sure?"

I nodded. "Yeah. Not from the pictures, but from her journals. She left Sugarleaf thinking the love of her life had died protecting her, and she never got over it. So knowing now that *you're* here, that he lived, but they never saw each other again. It's pretty..."

"Upsetting?"

"Yeah," I whispered, taking a seat beside him. "He made her promise to keep living, to go on without him... so she kept that promise as best she could."

Ellis blew out a sigh. "I guess he didn't know where she'd gone. And even if he did... he wanted her to continue with that promise."

"But she was *so hurt*. She never loved like that again."

"Him either," Ellis told me. "But he *loved* love for everybody else. Loved weddings – like I was telling you before."

I smiled. "Yeah. In her journals Hailey said he loved weddings then too. Said they hadn't really started planning yet, cause he was getting on her nerves wanting to be in the mix."

Ellis let out a bark of laughter. "That's hilarious. But... you know I'm gonna get on your nerves too, when it's time for ours?"

My eyes went wide over the certainty in those words, but...

"Yeah," I grinned. "I do. His love for weddings... it's why she went to the bridal business. It was her connection to him."

"That's beautiful."

I nodded, agreeing. "It is. So..." I sighed, turning to him to meet his eyes. "We're just accepting this? This is nothing to us, just normal?"

"It's not *nothing* at all, it's... mindboggling," Ellis said. "But... do I accept it? *Hell yes*. Because as far-fetched as it is... I don't feel like a single thing in my life has ever made more sense than *this*. Than me and you."

"I wonder if the other Ellis talked to the other Hailey like this," I said. "Cause if so, I see why sis was so caught up," I laughed, standing up.

Ellis caught my hand. "Where are you going?"

"Hold on," I said. "I have something else to show you."

I crossed the room to get Hailey's journal – the one my mother had given me – from the desk. There was a particular bookmarked passage there I'd read so many times now, I could probably recite it from memory. I turned to that page before I put in his hands.

"Right there," I pointed, settling next to him on the bed, propping my head against his shoulder. "Read that out loud."

Ellis gazed at me for a moment, then looked to where I was pointing... and read.

"*I do not know what the future holds for me. I can only hope that I have done my love proud. I could never bring myself to love another, but I have made a life that makes me as happy as the circumstances could ever allow.*

But it still feels broken.

Like a circle that is not complete.

That day on the street, when he shielded me from death meant to claim us both, I feel like something happened. When I touch that scar on my side, I feel his presence more than ever. Like the mingling of our life forces at that moment has stayed with me.

I hope it stayed with me.

Maybe in another lifetime... his heart will find mine.

And what should have always been, will finally be."

The end.

NOTE

I hope you enjoyed Ellis and Hailey's story!

Please consider leaving a review.

For notifications about new releases, sales, events, or other announcements, you can subscribe to my mailing list.

ABOUT THE AUTHOR

Christina C. Jones is a best-selling romance novelist and digital media creator.
A timeless storyteller, she is lauded by readers for her ability to seamlessly weave the complexities of modern life into captivating tales of black romance.

As an author, Christina's work has been featured in various media outlets such as Oprah Magazine Online, The Griot, and Shondaland.

In addition to her full-time writing career, she cofounded Girl, Have You Read - a popular digital platform that amplifies black romance authors and their stories.

A former graphic designer, Christina has a passion for making things beautiful and can usually be found crafting and cooking in her spare time.
She currently lives in Arkansas with her husband and their two children.

To learn more, visit www.beingmrsjones.com or follow her across
most social media @beingmrsjones

ALSO BY CHRISTINA C JONES

(Links and more info for all titles can be found on my website.)

THE CLARKE BROTHERS

Collision Course

Controlled Chaos

Close Contact

THE WRIGHT BROTHERS

Getting Schooled

Pulling Doubles

Bending the Rules

THE LOVE SISTERS

I Think I Might Love You

I Think I Might Need You

I Think I Might Want You

SUGAR VALLEY

The Culmination of Everything

The Point of It All

INEVITABLE SERIES

Inevitable Conclusions

Inevitable Seductions

Inevitable Addiction

THE TROUBLE SERIES

The Trouble With Love: a tale of two sisters

The Trouble With Us

The Right Kind of Trouble

IF YOU CAN SERIES

Catch Me If You Can

Release Me If You Can

Save Me If You Can

HIGH STAKES SERIES

Ante Up

King of Hearts: A Short Story Collection

Deuces Wild

EQUILIBRIUM SERIES

Love Notes

Grow Something: An Equilibrium Novelette

In Tandem

Frosted.Whipped.Buttered: An Equilibrium Short

Plus One: An Equilibrium Short

Bittersweet

Press Rewind: An Equilibrium Short

SWEET HEAT SERIES

Hints of Spice

A Dash of Heat

A Touch of Sugar

SERENDIPITOUS SERIES

A Crazy Little Thing Called Love

Didn't Mean To Love You

Fall in Love Again

The Way Love Goes

Love You Forever

Something Like Love

Wonder

Equivalent Exchange

Love & Other Things

A Mutually Beneficial Agreement

Relationship Goals: a novella

Anonymous Acts (Five Star Enterprises)

The Reinvention of the Rose

Me + Somebody's Son: A Heights Story

The Rose That Got Away

Subscribe

CPSIA information can be obtained
at www.ICGtesting.com
Printed in the USA
LVHW042130170522
718911LV00015B/811

9 781953 214256